Elizabeth found the scariest Halloween mask . . .
and it's turning her into a monster.

Beware of Elizabeth. . . .

Jessica reached out for her sister's face. Maybe if she could just see Elizabeth for a moment instead of that scary mask, she could—

"Take your hands off me!" *Elizabeth's voice rang out.*

Shocked, Jessica drew her hand back. "Elizabeth, you never talk like that," *she whispered, half to herself.*

Elizabeth laughed. "Yeah, right," *she said sarcastically.* "Well, you do what you want for Halloween. I'm glad I came up with this. It's way, way cooler than any lame-brained sea monster."

She sounds like me, *Jessica realized, putting her hand to her mouth.* She sounds like me on one of my mean days! *She forced a laugh.* "OK, Lizzie," *she said aloud.* "I guess I sometimes sound a little like that. Why don't you take off that mask now and stop the kidding around?"

"Kidding around?" *Elizabeth's voice took on a hard, cold edge.* "What makes you think I'm just kidding around?"

Jessica took a step backwards. "I mean—" *she began.*

"I mean, I mean," *Elizabeth said mockingly. She folded her arms.* "This mask is going to make everyone else wish they'd just stayed home Halloween night." *And she turned to go, her horrible laugh echoing down the hall.*

SWEET VALLEY TWINS

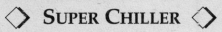

◇ SUPER CHILLER ◇

Evil Elizabeth

Written by
Jamie Suzanne

Created by
FRANCINE PASCAL

BANTAM BOOKS
NEW YORK • TORONTO • LONDON • SYDNEY • AUCKLAND

To Julian Decludt

RL 4, 008-012

EVIL ELIZABETH
A Bantam Book / October 1995

Sweet Valley High® *and Sweet Valley Twins*® *are
registered trademarks of Francine Pascal*

Conceived by Francine Pascal

*Produced by Daniel Weiss Associates, Inc.
33 West 17th Street
New York, NY 10011*

Cover art by James Mathewuse

ISBN: 0-553-48283-1

Published simultaneously in the United States and Canada

*Bantam Books are published by Bantam Books, a division of Bantam
Doubleday Dell Publishing Group, Inc. Its trademark, consisting of the
words "Bantam Books" and the portrayal of a rooster, is Registered in the
U.S. Patent and Trademark Office and in other countries. Marca
Registrada. Bantam Books, 1540 Broadway, New York, New York 10036.*

PRINTED IN THE UNITED STATES OF AMERICA

OPM   0 9 8 7 6 5 4 3 2 1

112183

One

◇

"Pumpkin bells, pumpkin bells, pumpkins all the way!" It was a Friday morning in October, and Elizabeth Wakefield was singing happily as she walked to school. "Oh, what fun a pumpkin brings for Halloween today!"

Her twin sister Jessica glared at her. "Honestly, Lizzie," she said with a sigh. "Can't you even keep your holidays straight?"

Elizabeth smiled. "Well, if you don't like that one, how about this: 'O pumpkin vine, O pumpkin vine, how lovely are thy branches'?"

"No good," Jessica said with a frown. "Pumpkin vines don't have any branches."

"I guess you're right," Elizabeth admitted. "How about this, then: 'O pumpkin vine, O pumpkin vine, I'll trick-or-treat as Frankenstein'?"

Jessica groaned to herself. Elizabeth could be so childish sometimes! A rhyme began to take shape in her head. "O pumpkin vine, O pumpkin vine," she recited, making sure she didn't actually sing the words, "take away this juvenile sister of mine." She laughed and ran ahead.

"What's so juvenile about Halloween?" Elizabeth asked, struggling to catch up. "I thought you liked it."

"Well, of course I like it," Jessica responded, waiting for her twin. "But what I like is *Halloween*." Her eyes shone as she thought about it. "You know. Scary, spooky Halloween." She dropped her voice down to its scariest and spookiest. "The full moon"—Jessica gestured toward the sky with her hand—"and wolves howling: Owoooo!" She hitched her backpack up. "Goblins and witches and ghosts—and I don't mean people walking around in an old sheet with eyeholes cut out of it," she added hastily, sensing that Elizabeth was about to say something.

"I like that stuff, too," Elizabeth said. "But what's wrong with pumpkins, and singing songs, and other things like that?"

Jessica faced her sister and sighed. "You probably like bobbing for apples, too."

Elizabeth looked surprised. "Of course I do. Doesn't everyone?"

Jessica turned and began walking again. "*Please.* I wouldn't bob for apples if you paid me. It's a kid's game." She rolled her eyes. "I mean, how old are you? Seven?"

"You know perfectly well I'm twelve," Elizabeth retorted. "And *you* used to like bobbing for apples. I remember—"

"That was years and years ago," Jessica said, interrupting.

"It was not!" Elizabeth stared at Jessica in surprise. "That was just last year."

Jessica frowned. "Oh. Well, what a difference a year makes, then," she said quickly, her eyes twinkling.

Elizabeth giggled. "For some of us, anyway."

"That's for sure. I know someone who's *never* going to change," Jessica said. "You!"

Jessica grinned fondly at her sister, who looked exactly like her. Both girls, sixth-graders at Sweet Valley Middle School, had long blond hair, blue-green eyes, and dimples in their left cheek. But Jessica was always amazed to see how different they were on the inside.

Elizabeth was quiet and serious, with a kind word for everybody—even for the twins' older brother, Steven. Though she made time for family and friends, she most enjoyed reading books and working on the school newspaper, *The Sweet Valley*

Sixers. Jessica, on the other hand, lived for gossip, fashion, and friends. She always wanted to be the center of attention, and she thought of herself as mature and sophisticated. She loved her sister more than anything, but sometimes Jessica thought Elizabeth acted kind of immature.

Like right now.

"I'm dreaming of an orange pumpkin . . ." Elizabeth sang, as the girls passed a house with a large pumpkin on the rail.

"Cut it out! You're embarrassing me!" Jessica said, giving her sister a gentle shove.

Elizabeth laughed. "There's no one around except us."

"Aaron sometimes walks this way," Jessica said meaningfully. She was talking about Aaron Dallas, one of the cutest boys in sixth grade and Jessica's sort-of boyfriend.

"Well, if you see Aaron, I'll shut up," Elizabeth told her. She began to sing again. "Halloween's coming! The pumpkin's getting fat! Please to—"

"Aaron's coming!" Jessica hissed at her. "Pipe down!"

Elizabeth stopped singing and followed Jessica's gaze. "Where, Jess?" she asked curiously.

"Nowhere," Jessica said with a grin. "I just wanted to see if you'd stop when I told you to."

"Oh, very funny, Jess!" Elizabeth pretended to

swing her backpack at her sister, who jumped neatly aside.

Elizabeth is so easy to tease, Jessica thought. *It sure helps that she always keeps her promises!*

"You know," Elizabeth continued, shaking her head, "one of these days I'm going to stop believing everything you say, and then what?"

Jessica smirked. "That'll never happen," she said confidently, as the girls approached the front door of the school.

"Don't be so sure," Elizabeth said, laughing. "Hey, have you thought much about a Halloween costume yet? It's only about a week away."

Jessica shrugged. "Not much."

"Remember when we went as a two-headed sea monster?" Elizabeth said, her eyes beginning to light up. "We had that long tail made out of papier-mâché, and we painted our faces green—"

Jessica stopped in her tracks. "I can't believe you're digging that ancient idea up again," she said loudly, in case somebody was listening. "I mean, talk about lame costumes."

Elizabeth turned to face her twin. "What do you mean, lame?" she asked, frowning. "Everyone said it was the cutest thing they'd ever seen."

Jessica let out a heavy sigh. Sometimes she was amazed that Elizabeth could be so smart and so dumb at the same time. "That's exactly the point,

Lizzie," she said in her most grown-up voice. "I'm in sixth grade now. I'm not some immature little kid any more. The last thing I want is for people to tell me I'm 'soooo cute'!" She imitated the voice of their next-door neighbor, who always passed out apples and toothbrushes to trick-or-treaters.

Elizabeth grinned, but her face quickly grew serious again. "We only did it two years ago, Jess. I mean—"

"Two years ago!" Jessica burst out. "No way!" She curled her lip and rolled her eyes. "We were, like, first-graders. At most!"

"No," Elizabeth said slowly. "It was fourth grade. I remember because that was the year—"

"All right, fourth grade, " Jessica interrupted, suspecting Elizabeth was probably right. "Who cares? I'm not doing a sea monster costume again, and that's final."

Anyway, she told herself as she folded her arms, *how can I possibly hold hands with Aaron on Halloween night if I'm stuck to my sister?*

Elizabeth shrugged. "OK," she said. "It doesn't have to be a sea monster if you don't want. But what if we go as a—"

Jessica shook her head vigorously. "No, no, and no," she said firmly.

"I haven't even told you what it is yet," Elizabeth pointed out.

"Look, Lizzie," Jessica said patiently. "The thing is, I just don't want to do another double costume again this year. It's kind of"—she groped for the right word—"kind of immature."

Elizabeth frowned. "Don't you even want to hear what my idea was?"

"Oops, there's the bell!" Jessica said quickly, just as the bell rang. She scampered up the steps of the school building ahead of Elizabeth, trying to ignore the look of disappointment on Elizabeth's face.

"'Scary night! Spooky night!'" Maria Slater sang out as she and Elizabeth headed for their usual cafeteria table at lunch that day.

Elizabeth wrinkled her brow. *What could come next? Aha!* "Halloween is really a fright!" she sang back.

"Great!" Maria set her tray down next to their friend Amy Sutton. "There's a witch who's riding a broom—" she sang.

"Better give her plenty of room!" Amy added. Elizabeth applauded, and Amy's eyes grew big. "I didn't even think about that," she whispered. "I just opened my mouth, and—it came out."

"Halloween will do that to you," Maria said with a smile. "Now all we need is a last line." She scratched her head.

"How about this?" Elizabeth asked. She'd just

had an idea. "Ghouls to shiver your bones!" she sang, and Maria and Amy joined in: "Ghouls to shiver your bones."

"You know, I think we're seriously talented," Amy said enthusiastically. "We should really write these down."

Maria took a sip of juice. "Good idea. Hey, Elizabeth, why don't you put some of our Halloween carols in *The Sweet Valley Sixers*?"

Elizabeth smiled. "Maybe. Oh, by the way, have you guys thought about what you'll be for Halloween?"

Maria shook her head. "I haven't had time."

"Me neither," Amy chimed in. "It's funny—it seems like when we were little kids, we were planning back around Valentine's Day or something, and now we put it off to the last minute."

"Yeah, I guess planning costumes isn't as exciting as it used to be," Elizabeth said, unable to keep her disappointment out of her voice.

"What's wrong, Elizabeth?" Amy asked, looking concerned.

"Oh—nothing." Elizabeth shrugged. "Well, it's just—"

"Tell us," Maria said, biting into her sandwich.

Elizabeth ran her fingers through her hair, and took a deep breath. "I wanted to combine with Jessica on a costume," she explained. "You know, like one year we went as a two-headed sea monster, and another year we went as a pair of tennis shoes?"

Amy nodded. "That was great. You kept getting tangled in each other's laces."

"But this year, Jessica says she doesn't want to do anything like that. She says it's childish."

"Childish!" Maria exclaimed. "What's so childish about a pair of tennis shoes?"

"I think they were Weeboks," Elizabeth said, thinking back.

"Well, you could make them Nikes instead, or Air Jordans," Maria pointed out. "I bet Jessica doesn't really think it's childish. I bet she just wants to get near Aaron Dallas—without you being around."

"Well, maybe—" Elizabeth began, when suddenly a thought hit her. "Hey! Maybe the three of us could do something together! I mean, since you don't have anything else planned yet," she added quickly. "If you think it's a good idea."

"I think it's a great idea!" Amy exclaimed.

Maria nodded excitedly. "What should we be?" she asked. "Did you have anything in mind?"

"Well, I'd thought of being a computer," Elizabeth said. "I thought Jessica could be the monitor, and I'd be the keyboard, and we'd have a telephone cord stretched between us."

Maria grinned. "Somehow I don't think Jessica's the most likely person in the world to dress up like a computer."

"Good point," Elizabeth admitted. "Anyway, that was a two-person idea, and there are three of us, so we'll have to think of something else."

Amy looked thoughtful. "What did they used to say on *Superman*?" she asked. "How he fights a 'never-ending battle for Truth, Justice, and the American Way'? Let's go as Truth, Justice, and the American Way!"

Maria shook her head. "People would have a hard time telling what we were," she pointed out. "How about Tweedledee, Tweedledum, and Tweedledumber?" Her eyes sparkled.

"From Alice in Wonderland?" Amy asked with a grin. "I like it!"

"I don't know," Elizabeth objected. She put down her fork. "The idea of 'Tweedledumber' sounds a little—well, a little mean."

Maria twisted her lips. "I hadn't thought of that, but I guess you're right. Can you think of anything else?"

Elizabeth chewed thoughtfully on a french fry. "Well, maybe we could all go as one thing—not three things in a set, but one thing that comes in three parts. How about—" An idea was beginning to form in her mind. "You know those department store mirrors that have three sides?" she asked. Amy nodded. "How about one of those? If we had a big piece of tin foil and walked next to each other?"

But Maria looked doubtful. "Wouldn't it be hard to stay together?" she asked. "And what about our heads?"

"Oh, right, our heads," Elizabeth muttered, picking up the cookie from her tray. "I guess that wouldn't work at all."

"I know!" Maria exclaimed. "How about we do a totem pole? We each make a mask. Then you get on my shoulders, Elizabeth." Maria's voice got more and more excited as she talked. "Then Amy gets on Elizabeth's shoulders and—"

"And Amy comes crashing down!" Amy said, grinning. "You couldn't support me and Elizabeth both, Maria."

Elizabeth took a sip of milk. "Maybe if we took turns being on the bottom?"

Amy shook her head. "Believe me. I'm on the Booster squad. We don't ever do stacks of more than two people. It's too much weight for the bottom person, and it's too far to fall for the one on top." She checked her watch. "Oops! Almost time for the bell to ring."

Maria stood up and began to stack her dishes back on her tray. "Well, let's keep thinking about it, then. Elizabeth, you're still having the party to-night, right?"

"How could I forget?" Elizabeth asked, bright-ening up. In fact, she realized with embarrassment, she had forgotten about it completely. She and Jessica were having a pre-Halloween slumber party at their house that night, and all their friends were coming. "Why don't you guys meet me at the front entrance right after school, and we'll walk to my house together?"

"That's us—the Three Musketeers!" Amy said with a grin.

"Hey, we could be the Three Blind Mice for Halloween!" Maria suggested happily.

"Or the Three Little Pigs," Elizabeth put in. The bell rang, but none of the girls made any move to go to class.

"How about the Three Bears, like in the story about Goldilocks?" Maria chuckled at the idea.

"No, no, no, I've got it," Amy interrupted. "We'll be the Three Little Kittens—you know, the ones who lost their mittens."

"Better yet," Elizabeth chimed in, "we'll be the mittens!"

Maria laughed as the bell rang.

"We'd better go," Amy said. "If we don't hurry, we'll be the three little sixth-graders in detention for being late to class!"

Two

"Last one to my house is a rotten pumpkin!" Jessica cried to several of her friends in the Unicorn Club after school that afternoon. The Unicorn Club was made up of the girls who considered themselves to be the prettiest and most popular at Sweet Valley Middle School, and Jessica loved being a member.

"Really, Jessica, that's so juvenile," Janet Howell said. She was an eighth-grader and the president of the Unicorn Club, and she considered herself to be *the* most sophisticated girl in Sweet Valley Middle School. But Jessica noticed that Janet was running after her, along with most of the other girls.

Jessica threw a look over her shoulder. "Better hurry, Lila!" she called to Lila Fowler.

Lila heaved a huge sigh as she continued

slowly along. "I can't run," she explained. "Doctor's orders."

Jessica slowed down in spite of herself. Lila was known for making things up, just to be dramatic, but you never could tell for sure. "Doctor's orders? Why?" she wanted to know.

Lila rolled her eyes and stepped gingerly onto her left leg. "Oh, she doesn't know exactly," she said, wincing as she put her foot down. "Whatever it is, though, it's probably very serious. I might—oh, ouch—never be able to walk again."

"That's really awful," Mandy Miller said, her face wrinkling up with concern. Lila took another step, gasping as she did so. "How long has this been going on?"

"Oh, a few months," Lila told her. "I just didn't want to burden all of you with my problems." She hobbled along awkwardly until she'd caught up with Jessica.

Since when? Jessica asked herself. *You've always told us all your problems before. Why stop now?*

And by the way, why weren't you walking like that when we left school?

"But what about your figure-skating lessons Lila?" Ellen Riteman asked, "I mean, if you can't walk—"

"Oh, figure skating?" Lila laughed hollowly,

dragging her leg along. "Figure skating's no problem. It's just walking I can't do."

Jessica caught Mandy's eye. The girls grinned at each other. Jessica was about to ask Lila more about her mysterious walking illness when Janet spoke up.

"Hey, Jessica, who owns this dump, anyway?" Janet jerked a thumb over her shoulder at the building they were passing.

"It's called the old Luna place," Jessica told her friends. She reached out to touch the rusty fence that surrounded the property. Looking closely at the old house, Jessica stifled a shudder. "It'd be a great place for a Halloween party, wouldn't it?"

"No way," Janet said. "It isn't spooky. It's just falling apart."

Lila laughed. "Look at the way the paint is peeling off," she said. "I bet the last coat was put on about five hundred years ago. Which reminds me. Did you all see the new paint job in my bedroom?"

"You mean the yellow stripes?" Jessica asked.

Lila rolled her eyes. "That was last month. Daddy got the men to come back. Now I have purple polka dots covering the walls." Lila's father was one of the richest men in Sweet Valley, and he gave Lila just about everything she asked for.

"How many times has that room been painted this year, Lila?" Mary asked curiously.

"Three, since New Year's Day," Lila said with a

happy sigh. She walked around Jessica to get a better look at the old Luna place. "I don't think even purple polka dots could help this place out," she added.

Before Jessica could point out that Lila seemed to be walking perfectly normally now, she saw something that filled her with dismay. Elizabeth, Amy, and Maria coming toward them, singing loudly. "Hark, the trick-or-treaters sing!" she heard.

Jessica cringed. *Why does Elizabeth always have to embarrass me in front of my friends?*

Janet curled her lip. "Are we going to have to put up with *this* all night long?" she demanded. She pointed at Elizabeth.

"That's right, Jessica," Lila said. "I mean, how childish can you get?"

"Pretty immature, I'd call it," Janet said, putting her hands on her hips.

"Hi, guys!" Maria called out, as she, Amy, and Elizabeth joined the Unicorns.

"Hi." Jessica managed a smile. "We were just looking at the old Luna place before we went home," she said, hoping Elizabeth and her friends would forget all about their song.

"Will you look at those colors?" Ellen asked, opening her eyes very wide. "Totally dreadful."

"Really." Lila sniffed. "Whoever lives there could use a good decorator."

"Speaking of colors," Ellen continued, "have you all noticed how well the purple on my new sweater goes with my hair?" She brushed her fingers along the sweater.

"Beautiful," Amy said, exchanging an amused glance with Elizabeth.

"No wonder they call it the old Luna place!" Janet exclaimed. "You'd have to be crazy as a loon to live here. Look at the rusty old lawn mower in the yard. Guess they don't even know enough to take it in out of the rain."

"The woman who lives there is supposed to be a real witch, too," Jessica put in.

"Jessica," Elizabeth said warningly.

"A *witch?*" Janet said in a shocked voice.

"Really?" Mandy's eyes widened.

"Really," Jessica said importantly, pleased to have everyone listening to her. "You might have noticed, there aren't many stray dogs in this neighborhood. They say she eats them—gobbles them down like candy."

"Jessica!" Elizabeth exclaimed. "Who says—"

"What else does she do?" Janet broke in.

Jessica looked mysterious. *Let's see—what else?* "Sometimes people say they hear screaming coming from the house late at night," she said, dropping her voice down low. "They say she snatches little children after dark and locks them in cages down in the basement."

"Jessica!" Elizabeth exclaimed more loudly this time.

"That's sick!" Ellen said, leaning closer. "Tell us some more."

Jessica's eyes sparkled. "Well—"

"Wait just a minute!" Elizabeth was facing Jessica, her arms folded on her chest. "Who says this? Who heard screaming? And what kids are missing from this block, anyway?"

Jessica bit her lip. "Um, well—"

"You don't know one single *fact* about the woman who lives here, do you?" Elizabeth said, challenging her.

"Sure I do," Jessica retorted. She started ticking them off on her fingers. "She keeps to herself, that's one, and she doesn't have a lot of money to spend on house repairs, that's two, and she doesn't have enough sense to bring a lawn mower in out of the rain—"

Ellen giggled. "That's three!" She held up her fingers triumphantly.

"That's not what I meant, and you know it!" Elizabeth said indignantly. "For all we know, she's perfectly nice." She looked at Janet. "And besides, it isn't called the old Luna place because of loons."

"Well, excuse me," Janet said, rolling her eyes.

"Luna means something else," Elizabeth continued. "It's Latin, or Greek, or Hebrew, or something like that. And it means—something to do with the stars, I think."

Jessica sighed impatiently. Of course, she knew *Elizabeth was right*. Elizabeth was almost always right. But sometimes she was just a little too—well, a little too *nice*. Who cared if they laughed at some old woman, anyway? "Come on, you guys," she said to her friends, as she began running down the block toward her house. "Let's go!"

This time, Jessica noticed, all the Unicorns ran along with her—including Lila.

Elizabeth watched the Unicorns running away, a frown on her face. "I totally think Jessica's the greatest," she said to her friends, "but sometimes she and those girls can be kind of, well, I don't know—"

"Kind of mean," Amy finished for her. "Do you think Jessica was just making it all up—about the woman who lives here?"

"Of course she was," Elizabeth said firmly. "She was just showing off for her friends, that's all."

But she couldn't help shuddering as she gazed at the old Luna place. The paint was a mess and the roof looked broken in places.

"Well, should we go on to your house, Elizabeth?" Maria asked.

"All right," Elizabeth agreed. She looked away from the house and noticed the moon floating in the sky directly above the roof of the old house.

How weird, Elizabeth thought. She blinked her eyes. Was she seeing things?

No—there it was again.

"Elizabeth!" With a start, Elizabeth looked at Maria, who was waving a hand gently in front of her face. "Earth to Elizabeth!" she said, smiling. "Are you there, Elizabeth?"

Elizabeth giggled. "Sorry. I guess I was a little distracted. I mean, did you see that?"

"See what?" Amy looked puzzled.

Elizabeth gestured toward the moon. "The moon."

"Yep, there's a moon up there, all right," Amy said. "A nice half moon. What about it?"

"It was as though—" Elizabeth began. "As though—" What exactly had she seen? She tried again. "It was like the moon suddenly swelled up to full," she said, thinking back.

"It just looks like a normal moon to me," Amy told her, glancing up at the moon again.

"Yeah. About as normal as they come," Maria agreed.

"Well, now it's perfectly normal," Elizabeth conceded. "But it wasn't a minute ago. Didn't you notice?"

"No." Amy looked curiously at Elizabeth. "Are you sure you're feeling all right, Elizabeth?"

"Fine," Elizabeth said stubbornly. "It swelled up right before that gust of cold air—" She studied her friends' faces. "You noticed that gust, anyway. Didn't you?"

Slowly, they shook their heads.

Elizabeth stared first at Maria, then at Amy. Frowning, she looked up at the moon once more.

OK, so it looks normal now, she thought. *But it didn't a moment ago, I know it!*

So why don't Amy and Maria know what I'm talking about?

Three

◇

"Slumber parties are the best," Jessica said happily several hours later. She was sitting in the Wakefield living room, surrounded by several empty containers of ice cream and what remained of a few bottles of root beer. "Are there any cookies left?"

"A few." Elizabeth passed her the plate, and Jessica helped herself to a chocolate chip cookie.

"So I've been trying to think of a good Halloween costume," Mandy said. "I have a bunch of ideas, but nothing's quite right. How about you guys?"

Jessica swallowed her cookie. She'd actually come up with an idea that afternoon, and she'd been waiting till the right moment to tell everyone. It looked as though this was it! "Well—"

"Guess what I'm going as," Lila broke in.

Oh, sheesh, Jessica thought with irritation. Leave it to Lila to barge right in. "Is it bigger than a bread box?" she asked grumpily.

Lila gave her a look. "Seriously, Jessica," she said. "Any *real* guesses?"

Elizabeth shrugged. "You're going to go as a dancer."

Lila clapped her hand to her head. "So close!" she said dramatically. "You must have ESP or something. But that's not quite it. Anybody else?"

"Um, a baton twirler?" Jessica guessed, growing curious despite herself.

"Uh-uh." Lila shook her head. "Nothing in my hands."

"A synchronized swimmer?" Mary guessed.

"Speaking of swimming," Janet cut in, "my horoscope this morning said I was as graceful and beautiful as a tropical fish."

"Nope, not a swimmer," Lila said, ignoring Janet. Her eyes twinkled. "But sort of in the water. At least, it used to be water." She pointed to her feet and grinned.

Jessica snapped her fingers. "A figure skater!"

"Right!" Lila beamed. "Good guess, Jessica."

Jessica smiled. She didn't feel like mentioning that she had guessed it so easily because she had also been planning on going as a figure skater. Typical that Lila should snatch her idea!

Janet rolled her eyes. "Anyway, as a beautiful and graceful tropical fish, I'll get lots of attention this month."

"Now, guess which figure skater," Lila interrupted.

"Oh, please, how many are there?" Janet burst out. "I'll get attention from a secret admirer who'll—"

"Remember Kelly Ireland?" Lila broke in.

"Kelly Ireland?" Jessica sat up quickly. Who didn't remember Kelly Ireland, last year's Olympic gold medalist? "You're going to go trick-or-treating as Kelly Ireland?"

"Better than that," Lila said with a smile. "I'm going to *be* Kelly Ireland."

Janet snorted, but Jessica thought she was beginning to look interested. "Just how are you planning to do that?" Janet asked.

"Daddy is buying me her outfit," Lila said, grinning widely.

"*The* outfit?" Jessica couldn't believe her ears. How many times had she seen that outfit on TV? "You're kidding!"

Lila shook her head, a smug expression on her face.

"What were you thinking about being, Jess?" Elizabeth asked curiously.

"Oh, nothing," Jessica said, crossing her fingers

behind her back. She wasn't going to be a figure skater, that was for sure! How could she compete with Kelly Ireland? "I know what we should do now!" she said suddenly. "Let's have a séance!"

"What a great idea!" Mary chimed in.

Even Janet looked pleased. "Let's do it!"

"This is going to be fun," Elizabeth predicted as she placed a single candle in the middle of the floor.

"How should we sit?" Mandy asked.

"Any way, as long as nobody tries to cheat," Amy suggested, looking hard at Lila.

"Hey, don't look at me," Lila protested.

Elizabeth laughed. "No one's accusing anybody, Lila. It's probably best, though, if we make people hold hands."

"That's not enough," Ellen protested. "We should hold hands and feet. Or else people are going to make noises by bumping their legs when the lights are all out." She wrapped her body into a pretzel. "See?" she asked. "Sit like this."

Elizabeth raised an eyebrow. "That looks hard, Ellen," she said. "Besides, I think it would spoil the mood. Why don't we trust each other?"

"Trust each other?" Ellen gave her a blank look, as though she'd never heard those words before.

Elizabeth felt very glad she'd never joined the Unicorns. "Let's just hold hands," she suggested again, joining hands with Amy and Maria.

Jessica took Mandy's hand, but she looked doubtful. "How about when people talk? How are we going to make sure they're really talking because of a spirit, and not just because they're trying to be funny?"

"That's easy," Mary Wallace said. "See, if a spirit is talking, the person's lips won't move."

"Really?" Elizabeth had never heard this idea before, but she guessed it sounded reasonable enough. "That settles it, then. Come on. No one's going to cheat, anyway."

"I wouldn't be too sure," Jessica muttered, but she took Lila's hand. "Light the candle, Lizzie."

Elizabeth let go of her friends' hands and lit the candle. Then she turned off the lights. The room felt a little spooky in the darkness. "Close your eyes, everybody," she said, as she slid back into her spot in the circle.

"How should we start?" someone asked. Elizabeth thought it was Mary Wallace, but she couldn't be sure.

"Let's ask the spirit world a question," Elizabeth said, with more confidence than she felt.

"I have an idea." *That was Janet*, Elizabeth told herself. "O spirit world," Janet continued in a strangely singsong voice, "send us a message from the Other Side."

"What other side?" Elizabeth could hear Lila ask.

"Don't be stupid," Janet told her. "You know, where the spirits are. I have it. O spirit world," she chanted again in her eerie singsong voice, "let us hear the shot that killed Abraham Lincoln!"

"Ugh, gross!" Elizabeth could hear Amy mutter.

"Jessica, close your eyes," Janet directed.

"My eyes *are* closed," Jessica insisted. "But I guess you wouldn't know, since *your* eyes are closed, right?"

Elizabeth stifled a giggle. She squeezed Maria's hand, and Maria squeezed back. It was actually kind of fun sitting there—even if there wasn't any such thing as the spirit world.

"Spirits, are you there?" Janet intoned.

All at once Ellen gasped. "I heard it!" she cried. "I heard the shot that killed Abraham Lincoln!"

"I heard it, too," Tamara Chase murmured.

Elizabeth opened her eyes. She hadn't heard a shot.

"I heard two shots!" Lila gasped, clutching at her throat and breathing heavily.

"Did two shots kill Lincoln?" Maria asked, letting go of Elizabeth's hand and staring at Lila.

"I heard *three*," Janet said proudly, as other girls opened their eyes and freed their hands. "It just goes to show you that some people are in touch with the spirit world and some people aren't." She looked pointedly at Jessica.

"Well, I heard a shot," Jessica said, folding her arms. "I'm as in touch with the spirit world as anyone."

Elizabeth sighed. "Come on, guys. Let's try it again." She held out her hand to Maria. "This time let's all concentrate on something. I know. O spirits!" she said, shutting her eyes. "Has anyone been killed on this very spot?"

"You know nobody has, Lizzie," Jessica said.

"It could have been before Sweet Valley was settled," Maria pointed out. "Let's wait and see."

The room grew silent. Elizabeth strained to hear any messages that might come from the spirit world, but there was nothing. She was about to suggest they try something else when suddenly she heard an unfamiliar voice.

"It's me—it's me—" the voice said.

"It's who?" Elizabeth asked, her heartbeat quickening.

"Me. I was killed here before there was ever a house—before Sweet Valley even existed—"

"What is your name?" Elizabeth demanded, tightly clutching Amy's hand.

"My name?" The voice seemed to be taken by surprise. "Uh—Kelly Ireland!"

Elizabeth snapped her eyes open. "All right, I

thought we were going to take this seriously."

"Yeah, who's the wise guy?" Janet asked impatiently. "Everyone knows Kelly Ireland's not dead."

"Oh, yeah—I forgot about that," Ellen said with a smile.

"Ellen!" Jessica and Lila groaned.

Ellen began to snicker. "You fell for it! I knew you would! I really had you going for a while there, didn't I?"

Jessica's cheeks turned red. "Next time you want to play a joke, Ellen, try to do it without your lips moving."

"And think of a good name first," Elizabeth added. But she couldn't help smiling. "All right. Let's decide now. Either we do this right—no fooling around—or we don't do it all. Which will it be?"

"Let's do it right," Amy answered. Mandy and Mary nodded.

"All in favor?" Elizabeth asked. All the girls raised their hands.

"OK." Elizabeth reached for Maria's hand again. "No tricks this time."

"Spirits, are you out there?" Janet asked a few minutes later.

Jessica made sure to shut her eyes tightly. She didn't want anyone accusing her of cheating. She listened carefully, but the only noises she could hear were Mandy and Lila breathing next to her.

"This isn't working," she heard someone say at last. It was hard to tell with her eyes closed, but Jessica guessed it was Tamara.

"Sssh!" Jessica couldn't quite place the voice. For another few moments there was silence.

"Sisters . . ."

Who was that? Jessica couldn't remember ever having heard a voice like that before. In her mind, she ran through the list of people at the party. *Not Amy, not Mary, not Mandy or Lila . . .*

"Sisters, beware!" The voice was sharp and had a strange-sounding accent. *Not Janet*, Jessica told herself. *And certainly not Elizabeth!* Jessica began to feel nervous. She opened one eye just a crack and looked around the circle.

"Who's talking?" That was Ellen's voice, all right.

"Sssh!" The voice had begun again. "Beware, sisters," it said. "Beware of the evil that will soon enter your lives."

Sisters? Jessica's eyes flew wide open. She and Elizabeth were the only sisters at the party. Did the spirit voice mean them?

"Close your *eyes*, Jessica," Janet snapped. Jessica stared at her. Janet's eyes were wide open, too. But before she could point this out, the mysterious voice began to speak again. "A great evil will turn a friend into an enemy."

It's Mandy, Jessica realized with a start. She dropped her friend's hand and stared at her. That is, the voice was coming from Mandy's mouth, but it wasn't Mandy's voice. *It doesn't sound like her at all,* Jessica thought, a queasy feeling at the pit of her stomach. She peered closely at Mandy.

Mandy's mouth was open. But her lips—weren't moving.

"Watch the rising of the moon," the voice continued, "and watch your sister. Otherwise, your lives will end in tragedy. Beware!" Mandy's mouth snapped shut. Her eyes were still closed.

Sisters? Jessica thought again. *Evil? Tragedy?* She glanced across the circle at Elizabeth. *Wait a minute.* The candle flame in the center of the circle was growing. Jessica rubbed her eyes in amazement. As she watched, the flame seemed to leap up toward the ceiling and become a glowing full moon. *The moon?* Jessica blinked in disbelief. At the same moment, she felt a chill wind. *There must be a window open somewhere,* she thought—and then the candle flame went out.

"OK, who's trying to be cute?" Janet demanded.

Jessica hastily got up from the circle and switched on the light. "Did you see that?" she said, her voice feeling a little shaky. "Did you see what the candle just did?"

"It went out," Tamara snapped. "Some idiot blew it out, I bet."

"No," Jessica said slowly, struggling to find the right words. "It was the wind. Didn't you notice?"

Ellen and Janet exchanged irritated looks. "What wind?" Janet asked crossly. "Really, Jessica, why do you always have to keep drawing attention to yourself?"

"Yeah, Jessica," Lila added. "Some wind! It must have been a storm—a storm called Jessica Wakefield."

"What will you think up next, Jessica?" Tamara added.

Jessica felt her cheeks heat up. She decided not to mention the candle flame swelling up to a full moon. She cleared her throat and faced Mandy. "What did you mean when you said that stuff about sisters?" she asked.

Mandy looked down at the floor. Suddenly, Jessica noticed that her face was weirdly pale. "I—" Mandy swallowed. "I don't know. I guess—I don't remember."

Jessica felt a tingle of alarm. "It must have meant me and Elizabeth. We're the only sisters around here." She looked at her twin. "What do you think it means, Lizzie?" she asked. "What kind of evil do you think the spirit was talking about?"

Elizabeth laughed and threw a sock at her sister. "Come on, Jess," she said, laughing. "It was a great joke, sure, but Mandy was only kidding. Weren't you, Mandy?"

"Um, sure," Mandy said, smiling weakly.

Jessica looked at Mandy once more. *She sure doesn't look like she's only kidding*, she told herself. Then again, Mandy was a great actress, and she loved playing jokes like this.

Besides, things seemed a lot less scary in a brightly lit room. Jessica had probably just been seeing things.

I mean, a candle becoming a full moon—come on.

Jessica grinned and shook her head. "Pretty good acting, Mandy," she told her friend.

Four

◇

"Did you know that Sirius is the brightest star in the night sky?" Steven Wakefield, the twins' fourteen-year-old brother, asked early Saturday afternoon. He, Elizabeth, and Jessica were sitting at the kitchen table eating lunch.

Elizabeth took a bite of her sandwich. All the slumber party guests had gone home, and she was still thinking about her Halloween costume. "Uh, no, I didn't," she replied absently. *What else comes in threes?* she asked herself. *Three peas in a pod? The butcher, the baker, and the candlestick maker?*

Steven frowned at her across the table. "And did you know that Alpha Centauri is the nearest star to us? Besides the sun, of course."

"Uh-huh." Elizabeth chewed her food thoughtfully. *Three Olympic medalists? Three French hens, from the Christmas carol?*

"You did? Really?" Steven pressed.

"Huh?" Elizabeth blinked her eyes and focused on her brother.

"I asked if you knew that Alpha Centauri was the nearest star to Earth. Besides the sun, I mean."

"Oh." Elizabeth sighed. It seemed as though Steven had been talking about nothing but stars for the past week. "No, Steven, I didn't know that." She dropped her eyes quickly, hoping Steven wouldn't ask her any more questions.

"*I* knew that," Jessica announced.

Elizabeth looked up, trying hard not to smile. "Oh, yeah?" "Yes," Jessica replied proudly. "*I* knew that Alpha Centauri was the nearest star to Earth. Besides the sun, I mean." She looked at Steven and tossed her head. "I bet even *earthworms* knew that."

Steven frowned, then turned back to Elizabeth, taking an enormous bite of sandwich. "Mmmf mrgle mrming blmm?"

"*What* was that?" Elizabeth said.

Steven swallowed. "I said, did you know that Betelgeuse is a red giant?"

"Beetlejuice is not a red giant," Jessica said loudly before Elizabeth could say a word. "Beetlejuice is a cartoon character."

"I didn't mean *that* Beetlejuice," Steven retorted.

"I meant the star Betelgeuse. You know, the star up in the sky?"

"Well, excuuuuse me," Jessica told him.

Steven snorted and turned his attention to Elizabeth. "How about you, Elizabeth? Did you know that?"

Elizabeth sighed again. "No, Steven, I didn't," she said. "Are you taking an astronomy course or something?"

"You bet." Steven held up the piece of paper on the table by his plate. "It's a star chart," he said proudly. "It shows all the stars of the Northern Hemisphere and all the constellations." He gave Jessica a sideways glance. "A constellation, for those of you who don't know, is a group of stars."

Jessica rolled her eyes. "I *know* that."

"Like this constellation over here is Cassiopeia," Steven continued, pointing to a place on the star chart. "'The Lady in the Chair.' Want to know how it got its name?"

Elizabeth glanced reluctantly at Steven's star chart. Normally, she'd be glad to learn something new like this, but right now she was more interested in deciding on a Halloween costume than finding out about stars. Unless . . . "Hey, do you know if there are any stars that come in threes?" she asked Steven eagerly. *Maybe Amy, Maria, and I can go as a constellation*, she thought.

"Well, Orion's Belt does," Steven responded, showing Elizabeth three stars together on the chart. "Orion was a hunter, see, and—"

"Who cares?" Jessica cut in, taking a handful of potato chips. "What's in that sandwich, anyway, huh?"

"Jessica—" Elizabeth began. She hated it when her sister was mean to anyone—even Steven, who often deserved it.

But Steven didn't seem to notice. "Salami," he said. "And peanut butter, three different kinds of cheese, black olives, a couple of pickles"—he stared at the ceiling—"and a piece of lettuce so I can tell Mom I had some vegetables today. That OK with you?" He thrust out his chin and stared at Jessica.

"What, no mustard?" Jessica acted shocked.

Steven snapped his fingers. "Oh, right. Mustard, too. I just forgot."

"So Orion's Belt is only part of a constellation?" Elizabeth tried to steer the conversation back to the stars. She peered at the chart.

"Right," Steven told her. "Orion has about a dozen stars, including Betelgeuse. Three of them make up Orion's Belt, but they're not a separate constellation themselves."

"I get it." Elizabeth nodded. She had to hand it to Steven. He sounded surprisingly knowledgeable. "Are there any others?"

"Why do you want to know, anyway, Lizzie?" Jessica asked.

Elizabeth shrugged. "I was just thinking about a Halloween costume that Maria and Amy and I could do—since someone here didn't want to combine with me," she added loudly.

Jessica blushed. "Yeah, well."

Steven ran his hand through his hair. "Well, I'll look if you want," he told Elizabeth, "but I don't think I'll find much. Most constellations really need six or seven stars at least. If you don't have that many stars, it's hard for them to make a picture, know what I mean?"

Elizabeth nodded. "I guess so. Thanks, anyway." She took a sip of milk. "Actually, I have another question for you, Steven," she said, "since you seem to know so much about the sky."

Steven sat up a little straighter. "Sure. What do you need to know?"

"What does the word *Luna* mean, exactly?" Elizabeth had been wondering about this all morning.

"Luna?" Steven repeated. "That's easy. It means the moon. Any other questions you want answered before I start charging for my services?"

Moon, Elizabeth thought with alarm. Suddenly, the memory of how the moon had swelled up yesterday came rushing back. "I do have another question," she said slowly.

"Shoot." Steven settled back and slurped down the rest of his milk.

"When's the moon going to be full next?" Elizabeth asked nervously. In her mind's eye, she could see the half moon swelling and becoming full. *Tell me it was full last night*, she found herself wishing.

"Easy again." Steven drew out another piece of paper from beneath the star chart. "This keeps track of the phases of the moon." Elizabeth leaned over to see better. "Right now, the moon is getting a little fuller every day—see?"

Elizabeth examined the chart. Each day had a circle, and in each circle Steven had colored in a section. At the beginning of the chart, the colored-in parts were crescents. The one for yesterday had exactly half the circle shaded. "So yesterday there was a half moon," she said.

"Uh-huh." Steven beamed at her. "It'll keep getting bigger and bigger till it's full. That's six more days. Friday. Halloween." He grinned widely. "Watch out for vampires."

"And—" Elizabeth thought for a moment. "And then it starts getting smaller again?"

"Yup." Steven nodded.

"I see," Elizabeth said, although she didn't. If the moon wasn't supposed to be full till Halloween night, what had she seen yesterday?

*   *   *

"Too bad Elizabeth had to run off to the drugstore," Steven said ten minutes later. With his teeth he tore open the plastic wrapper of a cupcake. "I was just getting into telling her about the stars. Hey, Jess!" He looked back at the star chart, and his eyes brightened. "Did you know that on the other side of the equator, in the Southern Hemisphere, the stars you see are different? Isn't that fascinating?"

"Yeah, fascinating," Jessica replied. The stars weren't really her thing, but there *was* something that she wanted to know. "Listen, Steven, have you ever heard of the moon showing up someplace you don't expect it be?"

Steven frowned. "*What* are you talking about?"

Jessica took a deep breath. "Would you think it was a what-do-you-call-it, an obstacle illusion? Or could it really happen?"

"*Optical* illusion," Steven said with a smirk. "No, it couldn't happen. The moon goes only one place, and if it shows up someplace else, then it's just an optical illusion." He wadded up the cupcake wrapper and tossed it at the garbage can. "Or maybe you're just flipping out."

"Yeah, you wish!" Jessica retorted, but somehow she still couldn't take her mind off the moon. She remembered Mandy's words: *Watch the rising of the moon.* What had she meant by that? Why was the subject of the moon coming up so much lately? Suddenly, Jessica thought of that creepy house down the block. "By the way, how come that old house down the block is called the old *Luna* place?"

Steven gave her a look. "Because the people who live there are all extraterrestrials," he told her. "Haven't you seen those moon men walking around with their little antennas?"

Jessica groaned as she took her plate to the sink. *I'd like to send* him *to the moon!*

At least he'd made it clear that what she'd seen last night had to be an optical illusion.

It has to be, she told herself as she left the room. *No way it could be anything else.*

But somehow she couldn't quite believe it.

Elizabeth hurried her steps toward the mall. She was hoping to get a costume idea from the stores down there. She was also hoping for some spare minutes to think about what Steven had explained to her.

He wasn't very clear, she told herself. But she had understood one thing for sure.

Last night there hadn't been any full moon.

Which meant—what? Her eyes must have been playing tricks on her. *That has to be the answer.*

As she passed the old Luna place, she noticed a small dog sitting on the sidewalk. "Hi there, boy," she said, greeting it. It stood up and wagged its tail. "What a funny-looking fellow you are!" she told it. The dog was pure black except for its face, which was orange. *As orange as a basketball,* Elizabeth thought.

The dog came closer, still wagging its tail.

"You're a quiet one, aren't you?" Elizabeth asked the dog, bending over and reaching out her hand. "Here, boy!" She made clicking noises with her tongue.

Then she noticed why the dog wasn't barking at all—it had something in its mouth. "What do you have for me?" she asked, stroking the dog's side. The dog opened its mouth and dropped something at Elizabeth's feet. She knelt to examine it.

"How weird," she said aloud. It was a mask.

And what an incredibly disgusting mask, Elizabeth thought, with a little shiver. She looked carefully at it as it lay on the sidewalk. It was a skeleton mask, by far the most gruesome Elizabeth had ever seen. It had a faintly greenish-yellowish tinge, there were scars all over the cheeks, and the teeth were spread in a horrible, grisly grin.

Elizabeth absolutely loved it.

"Where'd you get this, boy?" Elizabeth stroked the dog with both hands, but she couldn't take her gaze off the eerie mask. "Does it belong to you?" She glanced up. Then she blinked her eyes.

Behind the dog an orange-yellow moon was rising, just over half full. And for a moment, Elizabeth thought the dog's orange face looked just like the moon behind it—only larger and fuller.

Elizabeth shook her head. Compared with the mask, the moon wasn't that intriguing. "Can I have it?" she asked the dog. The dog only whined and curled itself up, as a chilly wind blew down the sidewalk.

"Does that mean yes?" Ignoring the sudden cold breeze, she reached out and touched the mask. Close up, it was even creepier—and even more wonderful. She stretched the rubber, examining every scar and gash, every ghoulish bone.

Just then the dog got up and began to trot away.

"Come back! Come back!" Elizabeth called out. "Here, boy!" She whistled, but the dog seemed not to hear. It squeezed itself under the fence to the old Luna place and vanished.

Elizabeth frowned, then looked down at the mask again. She felt a little funny just taking it—what if it belonged to someone? But no one seemed to be around, and she had no idea how to find its owner. *It's fate*, she thought suddenly. *The mask was meant for me to wear on Halloween.*

She forgot all about Amy and Maria. Her body tingled with excitement as she grinned at the horrible mask.

This is going to be the best Halloween ever!

Five

Later that afternoon, Jessica stared down at the list of possible Halloween costumes on her desk. Already, she'd crossed off "figure skater."

"It's got to be something beautiful," Jessica muttered. With a pencil she crossed out "Devil" and "Wicked Witch." *I have to do something that will top Lila,* she thought. *And something that will really knock Aaron off his feet!*

She ran her eyes down the list. "Angel?" she murmured. *Maybe. With plenty of glitter and a halo a mile wide!* She paused and put a small question mark next to "angel." *How about mermaid?* she asked herself. *Well, maybe. A sophisticated mermaid, though.*

In her mind's eye, Jessica could see Lila watching jealously as Aaron sauntered over to Jessica Halloween night. He would be dressed as—let's see—a rock star. No, a basketball player. *No,* she told herself with a grin, *he'll be wearing a tux. He'll be— whatever kind of a man wears a tux everywhere he goes.*

She hoped Aaron wasn't planning to be a clown for Halloween.

Or a sea monster.

Jessica shut her eyes as she imagined Aaron, handsome in his tux, taking her arm on Halloween night. "Your costume is the most beautiful of all your friends', Jessica," he would say in a voice that was both debonair and dashing. (Jessica didn't know exactly what those words meant, but she had read books that used "debonair" and "dashing" to describe handsome men in tuxedos.) "It's especially more beautiful than Lila's," he would say, and Jessica would smirk.

Lila would protest, of course, Jessica said to herself. "But Aaron, my costume is Kelly Ireland's actual skating outfit!" she said, mimicking Lila's voice. *Then Aaron would frown and sigh—debonairly, of course—and say, "Well, it fit Kelly Ireland much better than it fits you, my dear." He would say "my dear," wouldn't he?* Jessica asked herself. *Yes, he would.*

Jessica grinned broadly. *Then I'd say, "Have a good time trick-or-treating, Lila. Hope you don't slip on the ice!" And Aaron and I would hold hands and walk out to trick-or-treat all around the neighborhood, stopping now and then to gaze into each other's eyes and—*

Oops.

Jessica sighed and sat back in her chair. If she was a mermaid, how exactly was she going to *walk* anywhere? Hopping around didn't have the same romantic feeling to it, somehow. With a slash of her pencil, Jessica crossed "mermaid" off her list.

There was a knock at the door. "Come in!" Jessica called, sliding her list off the desk and out of sight.

The door flew open and a horrible face poked in.

Jessica screamed in terror. She covered her eyes with her hands, but the image wouldn't go away— grinning, crooked teeth, terrible scars, and a gruesome black and blue color mixed with blotches of bloody reddish pink. "Take it away!" she screeched.

"Sure gave you a scare," a voice behind the mask said.

Sounds like Elizabeth, Jessica thought with surprise. Cautiously, she opened one eye and opened up her fingers just enough to see her sister's body below the awful skeleton face. *Only a mask,* she told herself. *Phew.* She cracked her fingers open a little wider. She could still feel the blood pounding inside her head.

"That's some mask," Jessica ventured weakly. She dropped her hands and forced a grin. *Ugh,* she said to herself. *That mask really is the most disgusting I've seen since—well, since a long time.*

Elizabeth spoke again from behind the mask. "I'm sure glad we ditched that feeble sea monster idea," she said, spitting out the words "sea monster" as if they were poison. "What a stupid plan that would have been. Totally lame."

Jessica stared at her sister. *I take it back,* she thought. *It doesn't sound like Elizabeth at all. When was the last time Elizabeth used words like* lame *and* stupid? Frowning, she stared harder at the mask. "This is yours?"

"You bet your boots."

You bet your boots? Jessica thought, remembering last night at the slumber party. *Last night, it was Mandy talking, but somehow it wasn't Mandy. Today, it's Elizabeth, but it isn't Elizabeth.* She reached out for her sister's face. Maybe if she could just see Elizabeth for a moment instead of that scary mask, she could—

"Take your hands off me!" Elizabeth's voice rang out.

Shocked, Jessica drew her hand back. "Elizabeth, you *never* talk like that," she whispered, half to herself.

Elizabeth laughed. "Yeah, right," she said sarcastically. "Well, you do what you want for Halloween. I'm glad I came up with this. It's way, *way* cooler than any lamebrained sea monster."

She sounds like me, Jessica realized, putting her

hand to her mouth. *She sounds like me on one of my mean days!* She forced a laugh. "OK, Lizzie," she said aloud. "I guess I sometimes sound a little like that. Why don't you take off that mask now and stop the kidding around?"

"Kidding around?" Elizabeth's voice took on a hard, cold edge. "What makes you think I'm just kidding around?"

Jessica took a step backward. "I mean—" she began.

"I mean, I mean," Elizabeth said mockingly. She folded her arms. "This mask is going to make everyone else wish they'd just stayed home Halloween night." She turned to go, her horrible laugh echoing down the hall.

Jessica covered her ears as she watched her sister heading toward her own bedroom. *What's going on? That doesn't sound like Elizabeth at all!*

Get a grip, Jessica told herself ten minutes later, as she leaned back against the pillows on her bed. *That mask wasn't really all that scary.* She shut her eyes, so she could see it in her mind once again. The grin, the color, the scars . . . *Well, sure it's gruesome,* she decided. *But not terrifying. Oh, no. Not for me, anyway!*

And as for Elizabeth's behavior—well, Jessica had probably imagined most of that, too. *I mean, I prob-*

ably didn't even understand half of what Elizabeth was saying, because the mask got in the way. And no wonder her voice sounded all weird! Jessica covered her mouth firmly with both her hands, leaving only a little air-hole. "Halloween is my favorite holiday," she said, only it came out sounding a lot more like "Everyone eats mice except Polly May." Or something like that. Anyway, the voice she heard was *definitely* not hers.

Jessica breathed a sigh of relief. There was nothing to worry about.

But she decided to go see if Steven had noticed anything strange about Elizabeth—just in case.

"Look," Steven told Jessica when she walked into his room. "You can see the whole sky now that it's dark." He moved over and handed Jessica the eyepiece to his small telescope.

Jessica sighed loudly. "I didn't come in here to look at the stars, Steven, I came to ask you if you'd noticed anything different about Elizabeth."

"Uh-huh," Steven said, pressing the telescope up against Jessica's eye. Jessica backed away.

"Seriously, Steven, I only wanted to know—"

"Wait a minute, wait a minute!" Steven said, interrupting. "You're going to get a great view of the moon in a second. Now that it's higher in the sky, it's going to be so amazing! Wait . . . wait . . . wait . . . Now!"

Steven thrust the eyepiece right up at Jessica. She stared through it, but she couldn't see a thing. "A little more to the left," Steven was saying, grabbing the telescope and yanking it toward him. "No, a little too far—"

"Hey, let me look, OK?" Jessica said with some irritation. Taking a deep breath, she wiggled the telescope. She was feeling kind of jumpy all of a sudden, she realized. *It's only the moon,* she told herself. *You've seen the moon a million times. Take it easy!*

But she still felt nervous.

Bright light flashed through the eyepiece. "There it is," she whispered, trying to hold the telescope steady. "It's like half full, right?"

"A little more than half," Steven told her. "It's really awesome tonight, isn't it?"

"Uh-huh," Jessica agreed. The moon *was* pretty awesome. It was a beautiful yellowish color. Jessica peered closer.

What was that?

Before her eyes, the moon began to swell and bulge. Slowly at first, then faster and faster, the missing half filled in until the moon was completely full. "It looks like the candle flame did last night," she murmured, sucking in her breath.

"It what?" Steven looked at her curiously.

Jessica set down the telescope and looked out the window. There was the moon, all right—the same moon, just a little over half full, that she'd seen a minute ago. *It didn't swell at all*, she told herself reproachfully. She had just been seeing things.

Steven took the telescope from her. "What's wrong? Some extraterrestrials scare you?"

"Of course not," Jessica said defensively, rolling her eyes. "But, um, just out of curiosity, you're sure the moon can't go from part full to all full just like that?" She snapped her fingers.

Steven laughed. "Of course not. Weren't you listening when I explained that to Elizabeth today?"

"Not really," Jessica said truthfully.

"Right. I should have figured," Steven said. "OK. Well, the moon orbits the earth, so sometimes it's on the same side of the earth as the sun and sometimes it isn't. . . ."

Jessica sighed and sat down on Steven's bed. It was beginning to look as if she might be there for quite some time.

"Lizzie?" Jessica asked fifteen minutes later, knocking gently on her sister's door.

"Come in!"

Elizabeth's voice sounds like her own, Jessica thought happily. *I must really have imagined the whole thing.*

Jessica opened the door—and gasped. There on Elizabeth's bed sat the mask, just as horrible as ever. In fact, it was even ghastlier than Jessica remembered.

"Where'd you get this?" Jessica gestured toward the mask, afraid even to touch it. She picked up Elizabeth's pillow from the bed and casually dropped it on top of the mask.

"It's really neat, huh?" Elizabeth said with a smile.

"You could say that," Jessica said, grimacing.

Elizabeth reached out and picked up the pillow so she could see the mask again. "Oh, Jess, it was so amazing!" Quickly, she told Jessica about how the little black dog with the orange face had dropped it on the sidewalk and then vanished. She picked up the mask and stroked it. "This mask is so awesome. Halloween is going to be so much fun this year—I just can't wait!"

Jessica frowned. "But—don't you think you ought to find the owner and give it back?"

Elizabeth stared at her sister. "Why would I want to do a thing like that?"

"Well, because it's the right thing to do," Jessica said slowly, realizing that she sounded strangely like Elizabeth—at least the way Elizabeth usually sounded. *She's always telling me to do what's best for other people—even if it isn't best for me*, Jessica reflected.

Elizabeth grabbed the mask and pressed it up

against her chest, folding both her arms across it. "No way," she said. "This mask is mine!"

Jessica widened her eyes. "But it could belong to someone. Maybe it belongs to the dog's owner."

"That dog doesn't have an owner," Elizabeth argued, clutching the mask tighter.

"How do you know?"

Elizabeth shrugged. "It was a stray. I just know."

"Then maybe it stole the mask off someone's porch," Jessica pressed.

"It didn't," Elizabeth said firmly.

Jessica sighed loudly. "Come on, Lizzie," she said in exasperation. "That mask isn't the kind of thing you like to wear on Halloween, anyway. Why don't you just hang it on the fence of the old Luna place so its owner can take it back?"

"No way." Elizabeth stared defiantly at Jessica.

Jessica furrowed her brow. *I guess she really likes that mask,* she realized, looking once more at the ugly yellowish-greenish rubber. *Elizabeth sure has weird taste about some things.*

"Well, see you later, alligator," Jessica said, using one of Elizabeth's favorite expressions from when they were younger. She waited for Elizabeth to smile and say, "After a while, crocodile."

But Elizabeth didn't. "Uh-huh," she said absentmindedly. Relaxing her grip on the mask, she began to stroke it again.

Jessica gave her sister a long look, then walked back to her room. *Funny*, she told herself. *We've had plenty of conversations like that one before. It's just that—*

It's just that usually it's Elizabeth trying to convince me to do what's honest and fair, and today it was the other way around!

Though the house wasn't at all cold, Jessica shivered.

It's like Elizabeth's becoming—the worst parts of me.

Six

$\Diamond$

"Mmm, lasagna," Jessica said happily as she sat down at the kitchen table on Sunday evening.

Mrs. Wakefield smiled. "We'll eat just as soon as Elizabeth comes downstairs."

"Want me to call her?" Steven offered. He stood up from the table and loped over to the stairs. *"Elizabeth!"* he shouted at the top of his lungs.

"Ouch!" Jessica said dramatically, putting her hands over her ears. "His voice is even uglier than usual when it's that loud."

"Dinner!" Steven shouted even more loudly.

"I don't think she'll have any trouble hearing you," Mr. Wakefield said, raising his voice slightly. "Why don't you come to the table and tell us about your day."

Steven grinned and walked back to the table.

"Actually, I did some pretty neat stuff today—a whole bunch of sun experiments."

"Sun experiments?" Mr. Wakefield repeated.

"Don't ask," Jessica interrupted. "We'll be here all night!"

"Jessica," Mrs. Wakefield said warningly.

"Sorry," Jessica muttered.

"You wouldn't understand anyway," Steven said, waving his hand at his sister. "This is complicated stuff. Real science. High school science, not that baby stuff you get in sixth grade."

"Yeah, sure," Jessica jeered. "I bet I can understand all of it. Try me."

"OK," Steven said, smiling. "Like there's going to be a lunar eclipse on Halloween night. Know what that is, O Big Brain?"

"Of course I do," Jessica said, even though she really had no idea. "It's when the moon disappears—or something." She grinned. "Right, Little Brain?"

"Cool it, you two," Mr. Wakefield said. He looked at his watch. "I guess I'd better go get Elizabeth myself. What's she doing up there, anyway?"

"Beats me," Jessica said. She hadn't seen much of Elizabeth all day, she realized.

Mr. Wakefield got up and went to the stairs. *"Elizabeth!"* he bellowed. Jessica jumped. Her father sounded at least twice as loud as Steven had. *"Dinner!"*

"OK, you have the earth and the sun, right?" Steven said to Jessica, as though there'd been no interruption. "You also have the moon." He set up his plate, his glass, and his napkin so each piece was in line. "Usually the moon is over here"—he moved his glass out of the way—"so the sunlight hits it, no problem. Do you understand so far?"

"Uh-huh," Jessica lied.

"Really?" Steven looked surprised.

"Yes, *really*," Jessica replied.

"Well, once in a while the earth gets right in between the sun and the moon." He moved the napkin. "Then what do you think happens?"

Jessica smiled. "Then all the people whose initials are S. W. hop off the earth and go live on the sun," she said brightly. "Come on, Steven, I'll help you pack."

"Very funny," Steven said frostily. "No, the earth blots out the sun's light, and the moon turns invisible. That's a lunar eclipse."

"I like my idea better," Jessica told him.

"See?" Steven said. "You didn't understand that. Why don't you admit that the kind of science you do in school is just for babies?"

"OK," Jessica agreed. "The kind of science you do in school is just for babies." She turned toward her mother. "Can't we start eating. I'm starving."

Mrs. Wakefield frowned. "Isn't she coming yet, Ned? Tell her we can't wait much longer."

"*Elizabeth*," Mr. Wakefield began, "*if you don't—*" He turned to his wife. "She says she's coming."

"About time," Steven said.

"Funny, though," Mr. Wakefield said as he joined them at the table. "Her voice sounded kind of muffled. Maybe she's coming down with something."

Jessica froze. *Muffled?* she thought. *That can mean only one thing.*

Behind her, the kitchen door opened. Jessica turned around just as a horrible, awful laugh boomed out. She gasped and covered one eye at the sight of the mask.

"Oh, my goodness!" Mr. Wakefield said, sitting straight up in his chair.

"Spare us, spare us!" Mrs. Wakefield begged. She put the back of her hand on her head and closed her eyes.

Steven yawned. "She came down with something, all right," he said calmly. "Not a bad mask, Elizabeth. Where'd you get it?"

Jessica looked around the table. Her parents weren't really scared—were they? *No, they're not*, she decided. *And Steven's not scared either.*

She tossed her hair over her shoulder and stared

straight at the mask. *If it doesn't scare Steven, then it doesn't scare me, either!*

"Oops, forgot the lasagna!" Mrs. Wakefield said. She looked around the table. "Would someone mind bringing it over to the table?"

Jessica glanced at Elizabeth, who was always the one to help out. But behind the mask, Elizabeth didn't say a word.

Jessica bit her lip and turned toward her mother. "I'll get it," she offered, standing up and walking toward the counter.

"Thank you, Jessica," Mrs. Wakefield said, sounding surprised. "Be careful. The pan is hot."

Jessica grabbed two potholders and began to carry the lasagna over to the table. As she reached her twin, Elizabeth's leg jutted out right in her path. The next thing she knew, her feet slipped out from under her.

Splat! The lasagna cascaded onto the floor, and Jessica landed on her knees near the table.

"Jessica! Are you all right?" Mrs. Wakefield asked, getting up and hurrying to Jessica's side.

"Um, I think so," Jessica said confusedly. "But I've made a total mess."

Mr. Wakefield pushed his chair back. "I'll get some paper towels. Don't worry about it, Jess. I'll be right back."

"Better bring the vacuum cleaner," Steven called

to him, surveying the damage. "It looks awful. Hey, are you really OK?" He peered at Jessica.

"I'm fine," Jessica began, when she heard a sound she had never expected to hear in her life.

A maniacal laugh—and coming from behind Elizabeth's mask!

Jessica stared at her twin. "Are you—are you laughing at me?" she whispered shakily.

But Elizabeth only laughed harder.

"A tricycle? Are you crazy?" Amy looked carefully at Maria. *She doesn't look like she's crazy*, she told herself. *Still, you never know.*

Maria smiled back. The girls were sitting in Amy's living room after dinner Sunday night. "No, I'm serious," she said. "I think we should be a tricycle for Halloween. We'll all wear our Rollerblades."

Amy ran her fingers through her hair. "So we'd be, like, the wheels?"

"Right." Maria grinned. "Three pairs of Rollerblades, three wheels. Then we'll build a seat and a frame."

"Out of what?" Amy asked.

Maria shrugged. "Cardboard tubes, I don't know. We'll think of something. Just so long as we're all connected the way a tricycle is."

"I don't know—" Amy said suspiciously.

"We also need handlebars," Maria went on. "Whoever's in front will carry them. We could probably use cardboard for that, too."

"Or the top of my dad's stationary bike?" Amy asked.

"Sure, if he'll let us," Maria said. "Then all we have to do is skate down the street in absolute precision. We'll work out a really neat routine. It'll be like being in the Boosters."

Slowly, a smile spread across Amy's face. "I like it!" she said happily. "Let's call Elizabeth and—"

"Wait, wait!" Maria interrupted. "You haven't heard the best part yet. What do people usually say on Halloween night?"

Amy frowned. "Trick-or-treat."

"Not us," Maria said. "We'll say"—she paused—"*trike* or treat."

Amy laughed. "I love it!" she said, giving Maria a hug. "Now I *will* call Elizabeth." She dashed to the phone.

"Think she'll like it, too?" Maria asked.

"I *know* she will." Amy could hear the sound of the phone ringing, and then a familiar—though slightly muffled—voice. "Hi, Elizabeth, it's me. Amy," she said into the receiver.

"Oh, yeah?"

"We had an idea for Halloween," Amy continued, deciding to ignore Elizabeth's reply. "How does this sound: we're going to be a tricycle!"

Elizabeth snorted. "A *what?*"

Amy frowned. "A tricycle. You know, one of those things that—"

"I *know* what a tricycle is," Elizabeth jeered. "Have you gone completely out of your tree, or what? Of all the stupid, immature, and pathetic ideas for a Halloween costume, this one takes the prize."

Amy's chest tightened. "But Elizabeth—"

"'But Elizabeth,'" Elizabeth said mimicking her. "Why don't we all dress up as high chairs while we're at it? Get out of my life, Amy. Just get out of my life!" There was a click. Amy shook her head and hung up.

"What was *that* all about?" Maria asked.

Amy bit her lip. "It didn't sound like Elizabeth at all," she said in a low, dull voice. "She totally trashed the tricycle idea, and then she said—she said, '*Get out of my life, Amy.*'"

"She *what?*" Maria exclaimed. Then she shook her head. "You're right—that doesn't sound like Elizabeth, and I bet it wasn't. I bet it was Jessica playing a joke." She wrinkled her forehead. "Not a very nice trick."

Amy raised her eyebrows. "Do you think so?" she asked hopefully.

Maria nodded. "I wouldn't put it past her," she said. "Here, give me the phone."

Amy handed it over, already feeling better.

"Hello, Mrs. Wakefield?" Maria said into the mouthpiece. "It's Maria Slater. How are you?" She listened for a moment. "Um, Amy and I just called, and we wanted to know—were we maybe talking to Jessica instead of Elizabeth?"

Amy leaned in close to hear Mrs. Wakefield's reply.

"Oh, no, dear," she heard Mrs. Wakefield say. "That was Elizabeth all right. I just saw her talking on the extension right here a minute ago."

Amy's heart sank. "Oh," Maria said. "Well, thank you."

"If it didn't sound like Elizabeth, maybe it's because of the mask she's been wearing," Mrs. Wakefield suggested.

"The mask?" Maria asked.

"She's been wearing a mask around the house all weekend, and it makes her voice sound a little funny," Mrs. Wakefield explained.

"OK, Mrs. Wakefield," Maria said. "Thank you." She hung up and looked at Amy.

"I don't see—this is just so weird," Amy stammered. "Elizabeth has never talked like that to me before. She's never talked like that to *anyone* before." She looked at Maria pleadingly, praying she'd be able to come up with a rational explanation.

But Maria only shook her head, a disturbed look on her face. "It's weird, all right. And really, really mean."

Elizabeth sat on her bed, looking over her new vocabulary words. She'd dropped her mask next to her on the floor. Her ear hurt a little, and she rubbed it. *Almost as though I've been pressing it hard against the phone*, she thought. She laughed. *But that couldn't be, of course. No one's called me all day.*

"Famished," Elizabeth read from her list. She knew that word well. It was one of Steven's favorite words. She wrote "very, very hungry!" in the column labeled "meaning." After a moment, she filled in the "sentence" column, too: "My brother always says he's famished—even after Thanksgiving dinner!"

Elizabeth smiled. *Speaking of dinner, have I eaten dinner yet?* she wondered. It was kind of strange. She couldn't remember having eaten, but she wasn't at all hungry.

She glanced at the vocabulary list. "Lunar," she read. For some reason her body seemed to tingle when she looked at that one. *It means "having to do with the moon,"* Elizabeth thought, remembering what Steven had said. She was beginning to write it down when there was a knock on the door.

"Come in!" she called brightly.

Jessica walked in. "Hi, Jess!" Elizabeth said,

patting the place on the bed next to her.

But Jessica remained standing. "Elizabeth," she began. "Are you—mad at me?" She raised her eyebrows and looked straight at her twin.

Elizabeth smiled. "No more than usual," she teased. "Why? What have you done?"

"Are you sure?" Jessica stared so hard at Elizabeth that Elizabeth began to feel nervous. "You aren't still angry because of the sweater I spilled strawberry ice cream on?"

Elizabeth laughed and reached out her hand to her sister. "Of course not, Jess! That was weeks ago."

Jessica smiled slightly, but she didn't take her twin's hand. "And it isn't the headband of yours I lost, either?" she asked, rubbing her chin.

"You lost one of my headbands?" That was news to Elizabeth. "Don't worry, I wouldn't tear you to pieces over a silly thing like that."

"Well, good," Jessica answered. She relaxed her body a little and stepped closer. "And it wasn't the way I made fun of the old woman down at the Luna place, right?"

For some strange reason, Elizabeth's heart started to beat furiously. "No, nothing like that," she said, staring hard at her sister. "I mean, it wasn't a very nice thing to do, but I'm not mad at you or anything."

Jessica grinned weakly. She leaned over and

gave Elizabeth a hug. "Good," she said. "I'm really, really glad."

Elizabeth returned the hug, feeling puzzled. "Want to tell me what this is all about?" she asked curiously.

"Oh, nothing," Jessica said. She started toward the door. "I'm just glad to have you back."

Back? Elizabeth asked herself. *Back from where?*

She shook her head and returned to her homework.

That was a good conversation, Jessica told herself as she walked toward Elizabeth's bedroom door. She felt a lot better. Whatever had been going on seemed to be over now.

At the doorway she paused to look at her sister, who was hunched over her work in a pose Jessica had seen a thousand million times. Jessica heaved a sigh of relief.

Then she saw the mask on the floor, and she felt the blood rush from her face.

I know it's not possible, Jessica told herself, stifling a scream. *But I could swear that mask just winked at me!*

Seven

"I'll be ready in a minute, Lizzie!" Jessica called out, frantically brushing her hair. *Sheesh,* she thought, *it seems like every Monday morning is the same. No matter how hard I try, I'm always late getting ready for school!*

Jessica darted down the stairs. "Sorry," she told Elizabeth, feeling a little out of breath. "I'm really ready this time—I think."

Elizabeth leaned against the front door, an amused expression on her face. "If you're really ready, Jess, where's your backpack?"

"My backpack?" Jessica gasped, turning around. "I must have left it upstairs! Hold on one second, Lizzie. I'll be right back—I promise!"

Jessica took the steps two at a time. Her backpack was nowhere in sight. *Under the bed, maybe,* she told herself. Dropping to her knees, she checked. *Ugh.* A couple of old T-shirts, a sock or two, some wadded-up tissues, a fashion magazine she hadn't seen in weeks—but no backpack.

"Jessica!" Elizabeth's voice came floating up from downstairs. "Please try to hurry. I don't want to be late!"

"I'm trying—I really am!" Jessica yelled back. She brushed aside a lock of hair that had fallen over her eyes. *I'm so glad Elizabeth sounds like herself again,* she thought, checking her closet.

Still no backpack.

Where else could it be? she wondered. *Maybe downstairs, after all?* Jessica dashed down the steps. "Twenty more seconds, Lizzie!" she called out as she passed her sister. "That's it—I swear!"

She saw Elizabeth trying to hide a grin, and Jessica's heart soared. *I really did imagine the whole thing,* she told herself. *Elizabeth being mean, the mask winking, everything!*

The backpack wasn't on the sunporch. It wasn't in the living room, the dining room, or the bathroom. Jessica ran upstairs to check her room again. *If it isn't here,* she told herself angrily, *I'll—I'll—*

It was. "Oh, for goodness sakes!" Jessica grumbled, grabbing her backpack from her desk. She sprinted for the stairs. *At least I'm getting some exercise,* she told herself.

Jessica zoomed down the stairs and into the front hall. There she stopped short.

Elizabeth was gone.

Jessica looked around her in confusion. "Lizzie?" she called. *Maybe she's in the bathroom?*

Steven poked his head around the corner from the dining room. He shoveled an enormous spoonful of cereal into his mouth. "She left," he said with his mouth full.

"Huh?" Jessica stared at him.

Steven swallowed. "I said, she left. Walked out the door a couple of minutes ago while you were upstairs. Slammed it, too. Didn't you hear it?"

Elizabeth slamming doors? "N-no," Jessica stammered.

Steven nodded. "Good. Then she probably didn't knock down my telescope. If she's messed it up so I can't see the lunar eclipse on Friday, I'll pulverize her." He popped another spoonful of cereal into his mouth and began to chew it.

Jessica was struck by a sudden fear. "Steven, did you actually see her leave?"

Steven rolled his eyes. "Did I ever!" he snorted. "She was just standing there, and then she reached into her pocket and pulled out that mask she wore the other day—"

Jessica held her breath.

"—and then suddenly it was *Wham!*" Steven

continued, gulping the cereal. "And I swear, Jessica, if your sister's screwed up my telescope, I'm going to—"

But Jessica was already out the door.

Jessica ran as fast as she could. *Where are you, Lizzie?* she wondered, nervously twisting the straps of her backpack. She strained her eyes. Elizabeth was nowhere in sight.

As Jessica reached the old Luna place, she felt a sudden chill in the air. *Funny,* she thought, *it was warm when I left.*

There was a single light glowing in the attic window of the old house. With a start, Jessica noticed that the attic window was shaped just like a crescent moon.

But she didn't have time to get upset over windows shaped like the moon. All she knew was, she had to find Elizabeth.

Jessica rounded the corner. Now the air felt warm again. Up ahead she saw a familiar figure. "Lizzie!" she called. "Wait up!"

Elizabeth kept walking, not even turning around. "Lizzie!" Jessica cried again, a pleading note in her voice. She dashed across the street, scarcely even noticing the car that put on its brakes just ahead of her. "Elizabeth!"

Panting, Jessica caught up with her sister by the

end of the next block. To her dismay, she saw that Elizabeth's face was completely covered by the evil-looking mask.

"Why didn't you wait?" Jessica demanded, her breath coming in gasps. "And why are you wearing that horrible thing?"

"I happen to like it," Elizabeth said, her voice muffled. "What's the matter? You got a problem with that?" She walked faster.

"But—" As Jessica hurried to keep up, her foot caught a crack in the sidewalk. She lost her balance and lurched into Elizabeth, knocking her off stride. Quickly she reached out to catch her sister and steady her. "Oh, I'm sorry, Lizzie," she groaned. "Excuse me."

Elizabeth's voice was harsh and spiteful. "There's no excuse for you." She thrust her chin up high and kept walking.

No excuse for you? Jessica felt her cheeks turn red with shock. *Elizabeth had never, ever said such a thing before*, she told herself. *Never! Not even as a joke!*

"Lizzie—" she began, tears stinging her eyes. She wiped them away and reached for her sister's hand, but Elizabeth shook her off violently.

"You're such a klutz," Elizabeth continued. "You're almost as bad as Amy. No, I take it back," she added, shaking her head.

"You—do?" Jessica asked in a small, hopeful voice.

"You're worse." To Jessica, Elizabeth's words felt like a steel trap closing around her heart. "You're even more pathetic than Amy Sutton."

Than Amy? Jessica thought in disbelief. Other kids sometimes made fun of Amy. Jessica herself occasionally joined in. But not Elizabeth. Never! Jessica began to sputter. "Lizzie, what are you saying? Amy is—Amy's your friend—"

"Learn to talk English," Elizabeth said coldly. They had reached the door to the school. "Take my advice, Jessica," she continued. "Stop being such a wimp!"

She threw open the door and marched through. When Jessica tried to follow her in, Elizabeth gave the door a mighty push. It swung shut with a bang two inches in front of Jessica's nose.

Jessica stared at it dumbly. And when the tears began to fall, Jessica didn't even try to wipe them away.

"Hi, guys," Elizabeth said cheerfully at lunchtime as she approached the table where Amy and Maria were sitting. She had left her backpack, with the mask inside it, in her locker.

"Hi." Maria looked up for a moment and then glanced at Amy.

Elizabeth plunked her tray down with a laugh. "Is that all I get, just a 'Hi'?" she teased her friend.

"How about 'Oh, great! It's Elizabeth!'?" She opened her carton of milk.

Maria raised an eyebrow at Amy and turned to Elizabeth. "We didn't expect to see you here today," she said slowly.

Elizabeth looked at Maria with surprise. "Don't I always sit here?"

"After last night, we weren't sure you'd want to," Amy said sadly.

Elizabeth set down her sandwich and stared at her friends. "After last night? What are you talking about?"

"Well, after the phone call," Amy began, twisting a lock of hair around her finger. She paused and looked to Maria for help.

"What phone call?" Elizabeth was mystified. She pushed her tray away and examined Amy's face.

"The phone call we made to you last night," Amy said helplessly, not meeting Elizabeth's eyes. "When you answered and said—" She gulped.

"You called me last night?" Elizabeth tried to think back. She rested her chin in her hands. "I don't think so," she said slowly. Somehow it was hard to be sure, but she'd remember Amy calling her, wouldn't she? "Are you sure you talked to me?"

Maria sighed and smiled. "There's our answer, Amy," she said. Her whole body seemed to relax as she turned to her friend. "It must have been Jessica, after all."

Slowly, Amy's face lit up. "It must have been." She gave Elizabeth an affectionate smile. "I'm so glad."

Elizabeth was still bewildered. "Please tell me what's going on, you guys," she begged. "This conversation's going a little too fast for me."

"We called your house last night," Amy explained, "and Jessica answered and pretended she was you." She took a sip of her own milk. "We had an idea for a Halloween costume, but Jessica said some pretty rude things about it."

"Rude things?" Elizabeth frowned. "Like what?"

Amy turned red. "Well—" she began.

Maria shrugged. "Just plain rude things, that's all," she interrupted. "And what's really amazing is that she even convinced your mom she was you." She shook her head in disgust.

"She did?" Elizabeth was shocked. "That really doesn't sound like something Jessica would do."

"Well, put it this way," Maria said. "Either Jessica did it. Or else you're possessed by some kind of evil spirit." She smiled teasingly. "Are you possessed?"

"Well, no," Elizabeth said thoughtfully.

"I didn't think so," Maria went on. Her eyes

flashed. "So Jessica must be responsible. Believe it."
She took a bite of her lunch.

Elizabeth fidgeted with her straw. "Jessica probably thought she was being funny," she said, feeling angry and upset all at once. "But instead she
was being really nasty." She shook her head.
"Sometimes she just goes too far."

"Tell her after school," Amy urged. "We'll back
you up."

"I might just do that," Elizabeth said. *The nerve!*
she thought. *I wish Jessica wouldn't play mean tricks
like that.*

*It's just weird that I can't even remember the phone
ringing last night*, she thought, sipping her milk.
You'd think I'd remember that—wouldn't you?

But she didn't say anything.

Across the cafeteria, Jessica caught sight of
Elizabeth and smiled. *Good*, she thought. *She's put the
mask away, and she's talking to Amy. She was probably just
joking this morning. If I go over there right now, we'll have
a good laugh about what a good actress she was.* Jessica
stood up and picked up her tray. "See you guys later,"
she told her friends. They were all sitting at the
Unicorner, the official table of the Unicorn Club.

"We still have fifteen minutes left," Lila told her.
"And you never did tell us what you were going to
be for Halloween."

"Hmm," Jessica mumbled distractedly, staring across the cafeteria. "Oh, right, Halloween. Well, it's a surprise—you'll have to wait and see." And she hurried over to Elizabeth's table before her friends could say anything else.

"Hi, Lizzie," she said, reaching out to pat her sister on the shoulder.

But Elizabeth wriggled away.

"Get out of here, Jessica," Maria said icily.

Jessica felt a tingle of shock. "Get out of here?" she repeated. "How come?" She thought back to how Elizabeth had insulted Amy that morning. *Am I going crazy?* she asked herself, watching the two of them sitting together like the old friends they were. *Or is everybody else going crazy instead?*

"After that sorry stunt you pulled," Elizabeth snapped, "I'm surprised you have the nerve to ask a question like that."

"You were very rude," Amy said, folding her arms in front of her.

"I don't even know what's going on!" Jessica said, raising her voice. "What are you talking about?"

Elizabeth stared at her for a moment. "If you don't know—" she began. Then she sighed and turned her back to Jessica. Amy and Maria did the same.

"Well, all right," Jessica said at last. "I guess I'll

be seeing you." She walked rapidly toward the cafeteria door. *Great,* she told herself bitterly. *So I played some horrible practical joke on them, and I don't even know what it is!*

"I'm glad she's gone," Amy said indignantly, watching as Jessica left the cafeteria.

Elizabeth furrowed her brow. "I don't know, Amy," she said. "She really didn't seem to know what we were talking about."

Maria snorted. "It's an act," she said firmly. "It's got to be. Remember what Mandy said at the slumber party?"

"You're not taking that seriously!" Elizabeth exclaimed.

"Of course not," Maria said with a smile. "But Jessica did, don't you remember? And I wouldn't put it past her to play a joke like this just to see if she could help make the prediction come true. Remember?" She spoke in a low voice, imitating what they had heard at the party. " 'Sisters, beware!' " she repeated. "Then there was something about a friend becoming an enemy."

" 'A great evil will turn a friend into an enemy,' " Elizabeth quoted, a little surprised. It was kind of strange how she could remember Mandy's exact words.

"Whatever." Maria tossed her crumpled napkin

on her tray. "Anyway, listen to the great idea we have for a Halloween costume." Quickly, she explained the tricycle idea. "So what do you say? You'll join us, right?"

Elizabeth hesitated. "It sounds good," she said at last, "but there's this mask I was thinking of using for my costume—"

Maria waved her hand dismissively. "Well, there's no reason why you can't wear a mask and still be part of the tricycle. Right, Amy?"

Amy shrugged. "Why not?"

Elizabeth nodded. "All right," she said. "I'll think about it." But she knew secretly that she wouldn't. It didn't matter how great the tricycle idea sounded or that Amy and Maria were counting on her. She didn't want to be part of a tricycle. She only wanted to wear the mask.

Eight

◇

This is totally crazy, Jessica told herself Monday after school. *Nothing is making sense anymore. I've got to talk to Elizabeth.* She walked out the front entrance and stood on the steps, looking around for her sister.

"If I can just find her and have a good talk with her," Jessica muttered to herself, "I'll ask her what this joke is I'm supposed to have played on Amy and Maria, and I'll tell her I just plain don't like her behavior, that's all there is to it, and—"

A voice from behind her interrupted. "Whose behavior don't you like?"

Startled, Jessica whirled around and found herself face to face with Mandy Miller. "Oh, hi, Mandy," she said, forcing her lips into a smile.

"Come on, Jessica. You can tell me." Mandy's voice dropped low. "Which one are you talking about: Janet, or Lila? They're both getting on my nerves, too. Can you believe what Lila told Mary Wallace?"

"Lila?" Jessica repeated, as though she'd never heard the name before.

Mandy frowned. "Isn't she who you were talking about?" She stepped away from Jessica. "Of course, if you don't want to tell me—" She shrugged.

"Oh, no, it's not that," Jessica said quickly. Then she took a deep breath. She knew that if there was anyone she could confide in, it was Mandy. "Actually, it's Elizabeth."

"Elizabeth?" Mandy tilted her head to the side and stared hard at Jessica. "Elizabeth's the one you were talking about?"

Jessica nodded. "She's acting kind of—well, kind of rotten."

Mandy snorted. "Elizabeth? Rotten? I've got to see this."

"I'm not kidding," Jessica said sternly. "It's like she's—she's—" She groped for the right word. "It's like she's something evil."

"Evil?" Mandy put her hands on her hips. "We *are* talking about Elizabeth, aren't we?"

"Wait a minute!" Jessica had just thought of something. "Remember at the séance, Mandy?" she asked, rushing to get her words out. Mandy looked blank. "The séance," Jessica repeated impatiently. "You know. The one we had last Friday night?"

Was it only three days ago? "When you said that something evil would come into our lives?"

"What are you talking about?" Mandy asked.

She doesn't remember, Jessica told herself. A creepy sensation began to run through her body. Still, she couldn't stop talking. "You said at the séance that something evil would happen between two sisters. Yes, you did," she added firmly, as Mandy opened her mouth to object. "You said that something evil would turn a friend into an enemy, those were your exact words, and it's happening! My sister is turning into my enemy, and I don't even know why!" With a start Jessica realized that she was yelling. She looked down and saw that she had rolled her hands into fists.

Mandy backed away. "Anything you say, Jessica. Listen, I'm late for— I'm just late. Well, I'll be seeing you around." She ran down the steps without looking back.

"You did say that, you know," Jessica said softly as she watched Mandy turn the corner. "You really did."

She remembered how Mandy's lips hadn't moved that night. *Or at least your body said it,* she added to herself.

"Lizzie! Wait up!" Jessica had given up on waiting for Elizabeth on the school steps. She'd started to walk home, then spotted her twin ahead of her.

She must have left school by the back door. I wonder

why she didn't go out the front, as usual? Jessica asked herself, struggling to catch up. Elizabeth didn't turn around. "Hey! Elizabeth Wakefield!" Jessica yelled, a little louder.

That did the trick. Elizabeth turned around, and Jessica noticed with relief that the skeleton mask was nowhere in sight. "I've been looking all over for you," Jessica said reproachfully, as she finally reached her sister's side. "Listen, Lizzie, we really need to talk."

"What about?" Elizabeth asked. She swung her backpack off her shoulder and unzipped one of the pockets as she walked.

"I think you know what about," Jessica said. "It's because you've been so unbelievably mean the last couple of days." Jessica realized she sounded a little harsh, but she couldn't help it. "Do you know you're being so mean?" she added. "If there's something bothering you, Lizzie, we can—"

Jessica broke off as her twin took her skeleton mask out of her backpack and put it on.

That horrible laugh came out from behind the mask. Jessica winced. "Where do you think you're going, anyway?" Elizabeth demanded.

Jessica swallowed hard. "Home," she answered meekly.

"How come you aren't going to one of your stupid club meetings?" Elizabeth asked nastily. "I mean, has anyone ever told you that 'Unicorn' is an incredibly dumb name for a club? What do you do? Sit around and eat oats all day long? Hee-haw!" She kicked her leg out like a mule.

Jessica's mouth dropped open. "Elizabeth!"

"Oh, don't tell me," Elizabeth continued, pretending to yawn. "You just weren't invited. Your so-called friends are having a party without you. They're sick of you, that's all." Through the mask Jessica could see Elizabeth's eyes staring right at her—only somehow they didn't look like Elizabeth's eyes, exactly. "Or maybe they've borrowed all your clothes by now. Is that it?" Elizabeth went on.

"I—" Jessica began. She looked at her sister in horror. *It's like Mandy at the slumber party*, she told herself. *It's not just the eyes, it's the voice. None of it is really hers!* She almost wanted to check to see if Elizabeth's lips were moving. But she didn't dare.

"I—" she tried again.

"Typical idiotic answer," Elizabeth said, tossing her head. With one elbow she pushed Jessica off the sidewalk. "Get out of my way, loser."

Loser! Jessica was stung to the core. "Don't you talk to me that way!" she burst out. Then, before she knew what she was doing, Jessica snatched the mask off Elizabeth's face and flung it to the ground. Her fingers tingled strangely where they had touched the mask. Almost like an electric shock.

"What do you think you're—" Elizabeth began.

Then her face softened. She took a deep breath and smiled. "What's going on, Jess?" she asked gently.

Jessica felt weak and dizzy with confusion. "You were—very mean to me just now, Elizabeth," she said in a small voice, studying her sister's face. *Are you Elizabeth now?* she wanted to ask. *Or are you something else?* "I—I don't like it when you're mean to me."

"Oh, Jess," Elizabeth said. "I'm so sorry." She reached out and patted her twin's hand. "I'm so sorry if I hurt your feelings."

Jessica managed to smile, though her eyes had filled with tears. "Please—please don't call me that ever again."

"I won't," Elizabeth said. "Cross my heart and hope to die." She smiled. "Call you what, by the way?"

Jessica felt a rush of alarm. *She doesn't know why she's apologizing,* she told herself. *It's almost as if she's forgotten.*

Or like she never even knew!

But Jessica didn't feel like explaining—she wanted to forget the whole thing herself. "Come on, Lizzie," she said, pulling her sister along before she could pick the awful mask back up. "Let's go. We can make chocolate chip cookies or something, OK?"

"Sure," Elizabeth said. But she had broken away. Jessica whirled around and saw Elizabeth on the curb—picking up the mask and stuffing it into her backpack.

"OK, I'm ready," she said brightly, standing up and grinning at Jessica. "Let's go!"

But Jessica stood frozen with dread. As Elizabeth breezed cheerfully by her, she noticed the moon, just peeking over the horizon. *It's practically full*, Jessica thought with a shiver. It also looked, strangely, red.

At that moment, Mandy's words at the séance came back to her. "Watch the rising of the moon," she recalled the voice saying, "and watch your sister."

I'm trying! she thought desperately. *I really am! But I don't even know if I'm doing it right!*

"Unbelievable!"

Up in his bedroom, Steven fiddled with a few knobs on his telescope. "I'm going to be famous," he muttered. "Famous with a capital F!" He looked through the eyepiece. There it was all right, fading after a few minutes but still pretty clear: the moon rising blood red over the horizon.

I've never seen this before, Steven told himself happily. *I bet no one has. His astronomy teacher, Mrs. Nicholas, was going to be amazed at his discovery!*

They'll probably give me the Nobel Prize, Steven thought, reaching for his moon chart. Whistling to himself, he found a bright-red marker and tested it on the edge of the paper. *Not quite*, he thought, examining the shade of red. *Not—bloody enough*. To make sure, he squinted through the telescope again. *Definitely not bloody enough.*

Maybe if he added some brown? Steven picked up the brown marker and sketched a line on top of the red. *Not bad.* Using the red marker again, he started to color in the circle for Monday.

Of course, it's also a little weird, he thought. He cast his eye back across the first two lines of the moon chart. Each moon drawn in was yellow, or whitish, or kind of orange. Not a single one was blood red. For that matter, not one was any shade of red. *Well, I'll tell Mrs. Nicholas next astronomy class,* he decided. *Maybe I won't get the Nobel Prize. But at least she'll give me an A for the course.* Steven turned up the volume on the latest Johnny Buck CD and started shading in time to the music.

There was a knock on the door.

Steven sighed. "Come in," he called out. Jessica came into the room, a worried expression on her face. "Steven, can I talk to you for a minute?" she asked.

Steven sighed irritably. "Well, I suppose. I mean, I bet Nobel Prize winners never get interrupted in the middle of their science projects, but I guess it's understandable that you'd want my brilliant advice about something, since after all—"

"Steven," Jessica cut in, "I just wanted to know—" She broke off and looked at the floor.

"Let me guess," Steven said. "You're madly in love with a boy who's not as perfect as I am and you want to know how to fall out of love with him."

Jessica shook her head. "No."

"All right," Steven continued. "You wanted me to give you science lessons so you can become almost as brilliant as me." He sat back and grinned.

Jessica rolled her eyes. "You're not as funny as you think you are, Steven."

Hmmf. "You're right," Steven replied. "I'm funnier!"

"Ha ha," Jessica said sourly. "Listen, Steven, all I want to know is—" She stopped again and bit her lip.

"Look, Jessica," he said impatiently, "if you don't have anything to say, why don't you just, like, leave? I've got a ton of homework to do for astronomy class, all right?"

A look of urgency crossed Jessica's face. "That's what I wanted to talk to you about," she said with sudden determination. "Is it possible for the moon to rise looking all bloody red?"

Steven started. So Jessica had noticed it, too. He had to admit, he didn't like the idea that someone else, especially his little sister, had made the same discovery that he had. He didn't want her to get a complex about being brilliant or anything. "Of course it's possible," he told her breezily. "Happens all the time."

Jessica brightened. "Really?" she asked. "I mean, I don't think I've ever seen that before."

"Believe me," Steven said importantly, "it happens a lot. An awful lot. Of course, you have to know exactly where to look."

"Oh." Jessica nodded slowly. "OK, that makes sense. Thanks, Steven."

"Anytime." Steven leaned back again and shut his eyes. "You know me—always willing to help."

"Yeah, right," Jessica said, stifling a snort.

Steven's eyes snapped open. "I am too! You just have to approach me in the right way, that's all. Just say, 'Steven, my dear and wonderful brother, would you help me with this homework problem that I'm too stupid to understand all by myself?' and you'll get results, I promise."

Jessica snickered. "You wish!"

"Elizabeth does it," Steven argued.

"She does not." Jessica's face grew serious. "By the way, Steven, have you noticed any changes in Elizabeth lately?"

"Changes?" Steven scowled.

"Yeah, changes," Jessica said, staring at him. "Like being—nicer or, you know, meaner." She swallowed hard. "Or something."

Steven shrugged. "What are you asking me for?" he asked. "Elizabeth is Elizabeth, period. She's always been Elizabeth, and she'll always be Elizabeth." He sighed. "Don't get me wrong. Nothing against the kid, but can you imagine just going on being Elizabeth forever?" He shuddered and glanced at his moon chart. "Anyway, I'm much too busy with my astronomy to notice anything like that. Hey, you want to see something really neat?" He got up and walked to the corner of the room. "I made this really great model of the moon."

"No, thanks," Jessica said lightly, walking toward the door.

"What?" Steven exclaimed. "How can you say no?"

"It's easy, actually," Jessica said from the doorway.

Steven folded his arms. "Yeah, well, you'll be sorry when I get famous. I can see the headlines now: 'Great Scientist's Sister Never Bothered to Pay Attention to His Experiments.'"

Jessica laughed hollowly. "Why don't you try to pass ninth grade first?" she suggested, backing out the door.

"You'll be sorry!" Steven yelled after her.

He picked up the brown marker and finished shading in the circle on the moon chart. The brown and red mixed well. *Almost too well*, he thought as he put the cap back on the brown. *It looks bloody, all right!*

And compared with the rest of the colors on the chart, it certainly looked weird.

Suddenly, at the sight of the blood-red moon on his chart, Steven shivered. As far as he knew, no one had ever seen a moon like before.

So what made it red tonight?

Nine

Jessica checked the contents of her shopping bag. It was late Monday afternoon, and she was returning home from a trip to the mall. "Let's see," she muttered, "two carving knives, paper towels, and"—*where was it?*—"a package of Halloween stickers." *Corny, but it just might do the trick.*

After all, Elizabeth had always loved carving pumpkins. Each October for what seemed like forever, Jessica and Elizabeth had carved their pumpkins a few days before Halloween. When they were very little, Jessica remembered, they'd needed help from their parents, but for a while now they'd been doing it themselves. Jessica grinned as she pictured some of the great pumpkins they'd made: the one that had cooked spaghetti for hair (until the birds ate it), the one with the purple scar on its cheek, the one with the luminous marbles they'd borrowed from Steven to use for eyeballs.

Jessica had considered herself too old and mature to carve pumpkins this year. *But if it helps Elizabeth, it just might be worth it!*

"Anybody home?" Jessica called out, setting her shopping bag down on the kitchen counter. Then she remembered that her parents were out for the evening and that Steven was going to play basketball.

Jessica turned the radio on and took the packaging off the knives. She expected Elizabeth to show up any second, and she wanted everything to be ready.

Jessica rolled up her sleeves and spread some newspapers on the counter. Tapping her feet to the music coming from the radio, she got the pumpkins they'd bought last week and set them carefully on the newspapers. With surprise, Jessica realized she was looking forward to the pumpkin-carving ritual. *Maybe it's a little immature*, she told herself, *but no one said I had to tell Janet!*

Jessica inspected the pumpkins in front of her. The one on the left was definitely a little bigger and rounder. She turned the pumpkins over. The one on the right had a mushy spot near the bottom. *I'll let Elizabeth have the one on the left*, Jessica decided, turning the pumpkins back upright.

There was a sound at the door. "Elizabeth?"

Jessica asked nervously. "Is that you?" She set the roll of paper towels between the pumpkins and peered around the corner.

"Who wants to know?" came a sour voice.

Elizabeth walked into the kitchen, the mask firmly on her face. Jessica's heart constricted, but she tried to sound as cheerful as she could. "Look, Lizzie!" she exclaimed, flashing her sister her widest grin. "I got the pumpkins all ready. Maybe we can even sing some of your pumpkin carols while we carve!"

"Those dumb old things?" Elizabeth asked scornfully. "I don't sing stupid songs like that anymore."

Jessica looked at her sister pleadingly. "But just last week you—"

"And I don't think much of this little-kid music, either," Elizabeth said, stepping over to the radio and switching it off.

"Um—right. That was a stupid song," Jessica said, her voice trembling. She gestured toward the pumpkins. "The one on the left is yours. Why don't you grab a knife and start?"

"Are you out of your mind?" Elizabeth laughed. "I mean, of all the immature, pathetic things to do. Is this some kind of a joke, or what?"

Jessica's stomach knotted. She felt as though Elizabeth were plunging one of the carving knives deep into her heart. But she held a knife out to her sister, not wanting to give up. *Take it,* she thought. *Take it! Let's carve pumpkins, the way we did back in the olden days, when everything was fine!* Closing her eyes, she tried to send the message to Elizabeth's brain. *Let's be friends again,* she thought, concentrating hard. *Don't be mean, Lizzie. Please don't be mean!*

The door slammed. Jessica opened her eyes. Elizabeth was nowhere in sight.

"Don't wait up for me!" Elizabeth's voice came cutting through the door. Hysterical laughter followed, and Jessica heard Elizabeth open the front door. "If Mom and Dad would even let a baby like you stay up past six-thirty, that is!" Elizabeth added before slamming the door shut.

Her eyes full of tears, Jessica finished carving her pumpkin. She stood back and examined her work carefully. The eyes were big and round, with little ovals carved beneath them to represent tears. The mouth was curved down at the corners, and the pumpkin was turned so it faced Elizabeth's, next to it.

What's happened to you, Elizabeth? Jessica thought, sure she was going to start sobbing any moment. *What's happened to the sister I've known and loved for twelve years? It's like the girl going around in Elizabeth's body isn't really Elizabeth at all.*

I don't even know who she is, Jessica thought, blinking back tears. She looked at the pumpkin she'd wanted Elizabeth to carve. *She's a complete blank, just like that pumpkin over there. I can't even see her face!* Jessica took a deep breath, wiped away her tears, and brought her pumpkin out to the porch.

It was completely dark by this time, and Jessica's eyes took a minute to adjust to the blackness. Then she placed the pumpkin carefully on the porch rail. *It's going to need a candle,* she told herself. The idea cheered her up, somehow. She ran inside for a candle and a match. Opening the top of the pumpkin, she placed the candle inside and lit it. *Yes, that's better.* The flame leaped and cast a yellow glow through the inside of the pumpkin. The sad face seemed a little less sad and hopeless with that warm yellow glow inside—

Wait a minute.

Lit by the candle inside, the pumpkin looked like a full moon.

Jessica shut her eyes for a minute and shook her head vigorously. *Couldn't be.* She laughed. *Yeah, right, a full moon!* In the last couple of days, she'd seen enough moons to last her a lifetime.

Slowly she opened one eye.

It looked like the moon, all right.

Jessica blew out the candle. The pumpkin looked sadder than ever, but at least it wasn't the moon anymore. "Watch the rising of the moon," Jessica remembered. "And watch your sister." *For crying out loud, what had Mandy been talking about?*

Jessica heard footsteps coming up the sidewalk. She stared out into the night. Elizabeth! "Jessica?" came a familiar voice.

Jessica squinted to see better. *Good*, she thought. *No mask.* "Lizzie?" she ventured. "Come take a look at—"

"What?" Elizabeth took the porch steps two at a time. But as she looked around the porch, her mouth opened wide. "Oh, Jess!" she exclaimed. "You carved your pumpkin, and you didn't even wait for me! We always do it together!"

Jessica could only stare. "But—I—but—" she stammered.

Elizabeth looked at her with distress, waiting for her to continue.

"I wanted to carve the pumpkins with you, but a little while ago you—you—" Jessica broke off, not wanting to repeat what Elizabeth had said to her earlier.

Elizabeth's eyes were filled with pain and confusion. "I what?" she asked, her voice cracking a little. "What did I do a little while ago?"

She really doesn't remember, Jessica told herself, horrified. *She really doesn't remember what happened just a few hours ago when—*

When she was wearing the mask. At that moment, Jessica caught sight of the mask in her sister's pocket. *The mask is poisoning her,* she realized with sudden certainty. *It's making her into someone evil whenever she wears it, and when she takes if off, she forgets everthing that happened while she had it on.*

Jessica crossed the porch and gently put an arm around her sister. "I'm really sorry," she said softly. "I just—wasn't thinking, that's all." She gave her sister an awkward hug.

"Well, I wish you had." Elizabeth sniffled, but she made no move to push Jessica away.

I'm thinking now, Jessica told herself. She clutched Elizabeth harder with her right hand. With her left, she gently reached around her sister's back and groped for the mask in her pocket. *A little further—a little further—Ah.*

"You can carve your pumpkin later," Jessica said in her most soothing voice. "I'll help you, if you like." Slowly she pulled at the mask. It began to slide smoothly out of Elizabeth's pocket.

"I don't know." Elizabeth buried her head into Jessica's shoulder.

"If you don't want to, that's fine, too," Jessica added. *Hmm.* The last part of the mask seemed to be stuck on something. Frantically Jessica worked her fingers around it from the other direction. *There.* She raised the mask over Elizabeth's head and slipped it into her own pocket.

It felt like a weight had been lifted off her own heart.

"Why don't you go up and rest for a little while?" Jessica asked. "We're on our own for dinner. I'll bring you something, OK?"

"OK." *Elizabeth does sound awfully tired,* Jessica thought. She wondered if that was part of the effect the mask had on her. *Used to have on her,* she added to herself. Now that she'd gotten it away from Elizabeth, she was going to get rid of it, and that would be that.

Jessica helped Elizabeth upstairs and into bed. "I don't think you have a fever," she said, checking her sister's forehead. "I bet you'll feel better soon." *Will you ever!* she thought.

"Thanks." Elizabeth smiled up at Jessica. "Hey, Jess?" she murmured sleepily. "I'm sorry if I hurt your feelings about the pumpkins. I—I know you wouldn't have done it without a really good reason. OK?"

"OK." Jessica smiled at her sister and turned out the light. "See you later." As she left the room, she made sure to hold the mask so Elizabeth couldn't see it. *Just in case,* she told herself.

Coming back into the kitchen, Jessica hid the mask under a pile of old newspapers waiting to be recycled. *Tomorrow I'll bury it or something,* she promised herself. Feeling much better than she had in several days, Jessica went out to the porch and looked at the pumpkin she'd carved. It looked awfully sad, but she decided to keep it, just to remind herself.

She lit the candle again. The pumpkin still looked like a full moon, but somehow it didn't bother Jessica so much.

It's over, she thought happily. *It's all over.*

An hour later, Jessica rapped on Elizabeth's door. She held a tray with a steaming hot bowl of chicken soup and a folded peanut butter and jelly sandwich on wheat bread, just the way Elizabeth liked it. "Lizzie?" she called softly.

There was no answer.

She must really be asleep, Jessica thought with surprise. She turned the doorknob and peeked in. *That's funny. The light's on.*

Elizabeth wasn't in her bed.

"Elizabeth?" Jessica asked. Frowning, she took a step through the doorway.

Elizabeth was sitting at her desk. Then she whipped her head around. "Stop bothering me, loser," Elizabeth hissed through the gruesome mask that was once again covering her face.

Jessica screamed. Dropping the tray, she sprinted for the front door and out into the night.

Ten

Jessica ran and ran, hardly noticing where she was going. Her thoughts were a jumble. How had Elizabeth gotten the mask back? How had she figured out where it was? And what had made her go get it? Did the mask have some kind of power over her even when she wasn't wearing it?

Jessica's heart was beating wildly, and at last she couldn't run any farther. She leaned up against a fence. Her breath came in great shudders, and tears began to pour down her cheeks. *Elizabeth, Elizabeth,* she cried silently. *Elizabeth, come back to me!*

Her sobs grew louder and louder, but she didn't care if anyone heard. She cried harder than she had ever cried before, until finally, she was too exhausted to cry any longer.

Wiping her eyes on her sleeve, she looked up.

The air was misty and cold. The streetlights were glowing faintly. The moon was poking through the clouds. Was it her imagination, or was it larger and redder than usual?

Shivering from fear and the cold, Jessica decided she'd better go home. *If Elizabeth still has the mask, I'll—I'll lock myself in my room and play music as loudly as I can till Mom and Dad get home. Right. And I won't answer if she knocks on the door, no matter what.*

And if she isn't wearing the mask, then I'll find the mask myself. And then I'll—

I'll what?

Jessica realized that she didn't even want to touch the thing.

"I'll bury it in the backyard," she said softly, her words echoing in the empty, foggy street. *No. Elizabeth would dig it back up again.* "I'll flush it down the toilet." *No. It'd just back everything up and make a terrible mess.*

Then, what?

"Then I'll eat it," Jessica promised herself with a shiver. Determined, she took a step toward home— and touched something warm and furry.

For the second time that day, Jessica screamed.

I should call Elizabeth, Maria thought that evening. She was sitting on her bed, trying to do some reading for her English class, but she couldn't concentrate. *I wonder if Elizabeth's decided about the tricycle costume.*

Maria punched in the Wakefields' number. The phone rang four times, and the answering machine clicked on. "This is the Wakefield residence," Jessica's voice said perkily. "We're sorry that no one is here to answer your call, but if you leave your name and a *very* short message after the beep, we'll get back to you." There was a pause but no beep. "Except if you're a really cute guy," Jessica's voice went on. "Then you can leave as long a message as you like!" The beep sounded.

"Hi, Elizabeth, it's Maria," she said into the receiver. "Hi even to Jessica, if you're the one that gets this message. I guess I'm ready to forgive you. Oh, and sorry I'm not a really cute guy. Anyway, Elizabeth, call me back if it's not too late when you get home. OK?"

Maria was about to hang up when there was another noise on the other end of the phone.

"Anyone there?" Maria asked.

A muffled, angry voice came onto the line. "Maria?" it snapped.

Maria winced at her tone. "Jessica?" she guessed. "I'm trying to call Elizabeth, if you don't mind."

"Jessica?" the voice snarled. "What do you mean, Jessica?"

"You're not Jessica?" Maria frowned. *But if you're not Jessica, then —*

"This is Elizabeth, you idiot!" the voice declared. Maria gasped.

It's only a dog, Jessica realized as she looked down at the pavement. *Just a little dog*. Even so, Jessica found herself shrinking away from it.

"Nice boy," she told it uncertainly. *Are you supposed to reach your hand out toward a dog you don't know, or keep your hands behind your back?* she wondered. "Nice doggie." She couldn't remember, so she put one hand out and the other behind her back, just in case. "Good boy."

The dog whimpered and looked up at her.

"Are you hungry?" Jessica asked it, hoping it wouldn't decide to attack her. "Oh!" She started. The dog had a bright orange face!

Jessica stared hard at the dog. Her heart was racing. *This is the dog*, she told herself. *It's the dog that gave Elizabeth the mask!*

The dog whimpered again.

"What's wrong, boy?" Jessica frowned. The dog was turning around and walking slowly away from her. "Here, doggie, doggie, doggie!" She whistled. The dog stopped and looked at her, but didn't move in her direction at all.

This is crazy, Jessica told herself. *Here I am on a de-*

*serted sidewalk, trying to get a stupid dog to pay atten-
tion to me!* "Hey, boy!" she cried, clapping her hands.

The dog gave a low bark. Trotting away, it
turned its head around over its neck as if to say,
"Come with me!"

"You're totally nuts if you think I'm going to do
that," Jessica informed it. "After what you did to
my sister? What do you want to give me, a pair of
ruby slippers that will turn my feet evil?" But before she realized what she was doing, Jessica had
started to follow the dog.

The dog turned around and gave her a look. Its
face didn't look like a dog's face—it looked like a
moon. Prickles shot up Jessica's spine. "OK," she
said, shivering. "You lead on, I'll follow you."

The dog moved quickly through the streets,
sometimes so quickly that Jessica almost lost sight
of it in the mists. Once Jessica tried to catch up, but
when the dog began to run, she slowed back down.
After five minutes they were back in Jessica's own
familiar neighborhood—

Outside the old Luna place.

The dog stopped next to the fence, looking directly at Jessica. Behind the dog, Jessica could see
the towers of the old mansion. *Stay out of here,* she
thought fearfully.

But the dog was moving again. It slid gracefully
under the fence and stood on the other side.

That's funny, Jessica told herself. *It's almost as though it knew exactly where to go.*

Which means—

Jessica's heart thundered.

Which means, she told herself grimly, *that the dog probably lives here.*

Maria clutched the phone, not sure if she could believe her ears. "Elizabeth?"

"You want to do something about it?" Elizabeth's voice jeered.

"This—this is Maria," she stammered.

"Oh, please." The voice at the other end of the phone sounded disgusted. "Can't you get it through your thick skull that I have absolutely zero interest in talking to you and your other dweeby friends?"

"My what?" Maria suddenly felt dizzy. *This can't really be happening*, she tried to tell herself.

"What are you, deaf?" Elizabeth asked, her voice crackling with venom. " 'It's Maria Slater,' " she mimicked, turning Maria's name into a singsong. "Well, Maria Slater, will you please—that's p-l-e-a-s-e, in case you can't spell—hang up the stupid phone and get off the line? Betsy Martin might call."

"*Betsy Martin?*" Maria's head spun. Betsy Martin was one of the meanest kids in the school. Elizabeth had always done her best to avoid her.

Betsy's even too mean to be a Unicorn! "Yes, Betsy Martin." The voice sounded irritated. "Is your life so incredibly boring that you have to repeat everything I say?"

Maria bit her lip. *It can't be Elizabeth,* she assured herself. *It just can't be!* "Jessica," she said angrily, "why are you trying to fool me?"

But there was only silence.

Whoever was on the other end of the line had hung up.

The dog whimpered again and rubbed its back against one of the fenceposts.

Jessica sighed impatiently. "What are you trying to tell me, boy?" Her eyes flicked back and forth— and came to rest on a section of the fence that was missing.

"Oh, no," Jessica said aloud. "No way, José. You're not getting me to go in there!" She jammed her hands down into her pockets and turned around.

The dog whimpered again.

Jessica willed herself to put one foot in front of the other and head home. But she seemed stuck to the sidewalk. "Do it!" she hissed. Though her brain was working overtime, her feet weren't paying attention.

The dog gave a series of short yaps.

Slowly, Jessica turned back. As though in a trance, she stepped through the hole in the fence and into the yard of the old Luna place.

The dog led her around a corner and up to a window. Jessica shivered. *There are probably spiders in there*, she thought. The paint on the windowsill was peeling badly. Trembling a little, she pressed her nose up toward the glass.

Ugh. Spiderwebs.

Holding her breath, Jessica peered through the glass. At first, all she could see was darkness.

"Dog?" she asked. "Here, boy?"

There was no answering bark or whimper. Jessica looked down, but the dog wasn't where it had been a second ago. With a frown, Jessica looked left and right. No dog.

It had vanished.

Get out of here this instant! Jessica's brain shouted at her. But once again, her body refused to listen. Nervous and jittery, Jessica leaned closer to the window. *Whatever the dog is up to,* she told herself, *it must have something to do with this window. I wonder what's inside?* She strained her eyes to see.

Was that something moving? she thought, jerking back.

No—just the reflection of the tree branch in the breeze, she told herself, laughing nervously at her fear. Once again she braced herself against the windowsill and stared inside.

A shelf, she thought. *And a table.* She took a closer look. *Or is it a coffin?* Jessica wanted to shut her eyes tight, but she didn't. It was almost as though the old house had hypnotized her. *There's danger here somewhere,* she told herself. She could feel her heart hammering as her eyes became better adjusted to the gloom inside the house.

Crumbling plaster on the walls. A vampire bat! No, not a bat, she told herself quickly. *Just a coat, that's all. Nothing to be afraid of.* Jessica took a deep breath.

And a crescent moon.

"That's strange," Jessica said aloud, her words breaking the stillness of the night. It was comforting somehow to hear her own voice. "Now, why would there be a crescent moon inside—"

All at once Jessica's heart leaped into her mouth. Something was touching her shoulder!

Without daring to turn around, Jessica screamed—

And screamed—

Until a hand clapped itself roughly over her mouth.

Eleven

Let go! Let go! Jessica tried to yell, but it was no use. The hand had her mouth firmly covered. Instead, Jessica kicked backward, hoping to knock her attacker down. Her foot flew out—and hit nothing but air. *It's not alive,* she thought with a feeling of terror. *I've been grabbed by an arm without anything attached to it!*

Giving a mighty shove with her arms, Jessica strained to see what was over her neck. "Mmmm!" she commanded, trying to force her mouth open. "Mmmm!"

"Shh, shh," came a woman's voice from over her shoulder. "We don't want to wake the whole neighborhood, do we?"

Jessica kept struggling. *The voice sounds normal, all right,* she thought, *but it's probably just a trick. It's*

*probably an alien pretending to sound like a perfectly or-
dinary woman just so it can catch me off guard and gob-
ble me up.* "Mmmm!" she grunted, grabbing an arm
with her fingertips.

"Oh, my dear," the voice went on, "you must
think that I'm trying to hurt you!"

At those words, Jessica struggled harder.
"Help!" she tried to say aloud.

"Well, I wouldn't dream of hurting you," the
voice continued. "I just don't want you to bother
anyone with those noises. It's getting late, you
know."

Yeah, it's getting late, Jessica thought in a panic.
*Too late to be standing in front of a creepy old house
with someone covering my mouth.*

"My name is Corrina Black," the voice continued. "You can call me Corrina. Most of my neigh-
bors don't even know I live here, and I—well, I like
to keep out of sight." She laughed.

Jessica felt her heart beating furiously. *So this is
the woman who lives here,* she thought, *the woman who
looks like a witch, and I'm about to become her dinner.*

"Let's make a deal, then," Corrina went on. "I'll
let you go if you promise not to scream anymore.
Then we'll go inside, if you like, and you can tell
me what you want. Deal?"

What choice do I have? Jessica wondered. She
nodded.

"Good," Corrina said with a laugh, removing her hand from Jessica's mouth.

Her body numb with fear, Jessica turned around.

Corrina had long, long black hair hanging below her waist. Her bright-green eyes shone in the moonlight—*just like a cat's*, Jessica couldn't help thinking. She was gaunt and bony, yet there was something friendly about her face—way friendlier than she imagined witches looked. *How old are you?* Jessica wondered. She couldn't even begin to guess.

"So you live here," Jessica said cautiously.

Corrina laughed, a little more shyly this time. "Yes."

"Some people say you're a witch." Jessica spoke slowly.

"Do they?" Corrina's bright-green eyes burned into Jessica's own. She smiled.

Tell me you're not a witch, Jessica pleaded silently. Just in case, she took a step back. Bumping against the house, she gasped. "Oooh!"

"Why don't we go inside," Corrina suggested. "It's—" Her eyes sparkled. "It's cleaner than you think."

"No cobwebs?" Jessica wanted to know.

"Well, a few." Corrina reached for Jessica's hand. "Come on. Let's go. I'll show you the way."

Don't do it! Don't do it! Jessica warned herself. But once more, her body disobeyed. Corrina led her through a rusty screen door and inside the old Luna place.

The living room was definitely cleaner than Jessica had expected—a little cleaner, anyway. "Sit down," Corrina said, pointing to an old green sofa with horsehair pillows. Jessica checked the cushions for cobwebs before she sat down. *No cobwebs,* she thought, *but plenty of dust!*

"I haven't vacuumed in what seems like centuries!" Corrina explained with a pleasant laugh. "Can I get you something to drink?"

"No, thank you," Jessica replied, though actually her throat was as dry as sandpaper.

"Are you sure about that?" Corrina pressed, smiling kindly.

Jessica blinked. *It's like she knows what I'm thinking.* "Well—yes. Yes, please."

"I'll be right back," Corrina told Jessica. "Make yourself at home." She disappeared around a corner.

Make myself at home, Jessica thought, wrinkling her nose. Yeah, right. *Doesn't Corrina believe in lightbulbs?* The only light in the room came from a few candles.

Jessica glanced toward the center of the room and drew in her breath. A two-foot-high crescent moon stood on the polished surface of a small table. The moon was carved into a grinning face. "So I really did see a moon in here," she muttered to herself. She pried her eyes away.

Behind the table were shelves and shelves lined with old, old books. Jessica looked for a television set or a computer, but she didn't see any. *Maybe she doesn't even have electricity,* she mused.

Above the mantelpiece were four framed portraits. Jessica squinted. Then she got up and moved closer to get a better look. The first painting showed a man in a high white collar, a stern expression on his face. Next to him was a painting of a woman, her hair pulled back severely into a bun. Her dress looked incredibly old-fashioned. Jessica thought she had seen a picture once of her own great-grandmother wearing a dress that looked almost exactly like it. *I wonder if these are Corrina's great-grandparents?*

The third portrait showed a beautiful girl with a sunny smile. Her blond hair tumbled down off her face, and there was a sparkle in her eye. Jessica peered a little closer and felt another shock of recognition. *She looks a little like Elizabeth!* "Or me," she added out loud. She decided that the girl in the picture couldn't be much older than sixteen. *We could look like that in another four years,* she decided, examining the portrait critically. *I wonder if she's related to us somehow?*

But the fourth portrait was the most interesting. "It's Corrina," Jessica told herself, staring hard. Though the girl in the picture looked as if she was only about Jessica's age, there was no mistaking it: the long black hair, the thin face, the friendly expression. The painter had captured Corrina's flashing green eyes perfectly. Jessica began to feel a nervous sensation in the back of her neck. *How old is this picture, anyway?* she wanted to know. She ran her finger lightly along the frame. It came away covered with dust.

Ancient.

Beneath the dust, the frame looked old, too. And if the picture had been around that long, that would make Corrina—how old?

Jessica shuddered. Older than any living person ought to be, that was for sure!

"I see you're admiring my family," Corrina observed, coming back into the room. Jessica whirled around, startled. *She moves awfully quietly,* she thought, catching her breath. *Just like a—*

Like a cat.

Corrina chuckled as Jessica, blushing, returned to the couch. "Yes, that's me on the end there, when I was twelve," she told Jessica. Her eyes flicked from one painting to the next. "And my sister, and my parents. Here. I brought you a drink."

"Of what?" Jessica asked eyeing the bottle nervously. Maybe it was some kind of horrible-smelling witch's brew.

Corrina smiled. "Do you like iced tea?" she asked, handing Jessica the bottle.

"Oh. Yes, thank you." Jessica eyed the bottle suspiciously. Was it really just iced tea? She sniffed the lid. "What's in it?"

"Read the label," Corrina suggested with a laugh. "Tea, corn syrup, and water, I should think. Perhaps some citric acid. The things they do to tea nowadays!"

"Oh." Jessica checked the label and blushed. Changing the subject, she pointed to the crescent moon. "What's that for, Miss Black?"

"Corrina, please." Corrina sat on a straight-backed chair with a cracked leg and took a sip of her own tea. "That's a storyteller's symbol. It's recognized all over the world. Where there's a crescent moon, there's a storyteller. Do you see?"

"Uh-huh." Cautiously, Jessica took a sip of the iced tea. *Yep, it tastes like regular iced tea,* she thought with relief. "Are you a storyteller, then—Corrina?"

Corrina's face darkened. "You might say that." She set her bottle of tea down with a thump next to the crescent. "But I think you're the one with a story to tell tonight," she added, staring pointedly at Jessica. "Am I right?"

Jessica stared. "I guess you're right," she said

slowly. She sat up straighter on the sofa. "I haven't told anyone about—this." She wasn't sure why, but suddenly she wanted to tell Corrina about Elizabeth and the horrible mask. Corrina seemed kind, and also very wise. Only Jessica didn't know if she could get the words out.

Corrina smiled at her sympathetically. "It's all right," she said soothingly. "Have another sip of tea, and take your time. I won't try to rush you. Cross my heart."

Jessica swallowed some more tea, took a deep breath, and began.

When the story was over, Corrina sat in silence, her hands folded in her lap, her green eyes focused on something in the distance. Jessica tried to follow her gaze. It looked as though she were staring up at the family portraits over the mantelpiece, but in the flickering candlelight, it was hard to be sure.

"So—" Jessica prompted, breaking the quiet. "So do you have any ideas for me?" She cleared her throat. "I mean, do you know where the mask came from or—or what it wants?"

Corrina sat staring, as though she were in a trance. She shook her head slightly. "No," she whispered. "No, it can't be."

"What?" Jessica leaned forward, speaking louder in her impatience. "What's wrong,

Corrina?" As she spoke, she felt a chilly wind in her face. It seemed to be coming from the crescent moon on the table. "Tell me."

"That mask had been buried for forty years," Corrina whispered, half to herself.

Jessica felt a sinking feeling in the pit of her stomach. "Why?" she asked, afraid that she already knew the answer.

"Because—" Corrina paused and licked her lips nervously with a long pink tongue. "Because the mask carries a deadly curse."

Jessica felt her heart sink. Now she was sure of it—the mask was doing something terrible to Elizabeth. *I have to do something,* she thought, her mind racing. "How can I get rid of the curse and save Elizabeth?" she asked aloud, her eyes begging Corrina to give her an answer.

Corrina shook her head. "I'm afraid defeating the curse is beyond my powers."

"It can't be! There must be something you can do!" Jessica cried, springing up from the sofa. Once more, she felt like crying. "I know! If I steal the mask again, and bury it— Maybe you can tell me where it was buried before?" Jessica's fists clenched and unclenched. "Or if I take it far enough away, it can't possibly come back again—can it?" she asked hopefully.

Corrina looked at her helplessly. "Perhaps you're right."

"But you don't—you don't think I am." Jessica sank back into her seat.

"No, I don't," Corrina said gently. "And there's another thing, too." She reached out a bony hand to touch Jessica's knee. "The mask can take hold of the wearer forever—if it is worn long enough."

Jessica gasped. The words seemed to bore right through her heart. "You—you mean that after a while it wouldn't help even if I buried it?" she asked, swallowing hard.

Corrina looked grim. "I'm sorry. The more Elizabeth wears the mask, the more it will take control of her."

"Then I've got to do something," Jessica said. She forced her body to be calm. "Or is it—" An awful thought had just struck her. "Oh, Corrina, is it already too late?"

"I don't think so," Corrina assured her. "From what you tell me, I believe you still have a few more days." Jessica sighed with relief, but Corrina quickly cut in. "However, I'm afraid that's all."

Jessica's mind reeled. *Cut it into tiny pieces. Feed it to the neighbor's dog. Take it to the post office and mail it to Siberia. Something. Anything!* "Thank you so much for the tea, Corrina," she said, her words a jumble. "I have to—"

"There is one thing more," Corrina cut in.

"What is it?" Jessica asked, not wanting to listen to the answer.

"Watch the rising of the moon," Corrina said, her voice soft but intense. Jessica shuddered. *That's what Mandy said*, she remembered. "If your sister wears the mask through the rising of the moon, that will hasten the time when the mask takes full possession of her."

Jessica's whole body went cold. She thought back to the afternoon. "Today I pulled the mask off her face just as the moon rose," she told Corrina.

Corrina nodded gravely. "A good thing. You did well."

"Thank you, Corrina." Jessica drank the last bit of her tea and dashed for the door. "Thanks for everything. I've—got to go. See you around!"

Jessica tore around the corner and back out the door. Through the window she could just see Corrina sitting in her broken chair, staring sadly at the pictures of her family.

The house was dark when Jessica arrived home. Silently, she tiptoed up to the second floor. *Where's the mask?* she wondered. She had no clear idea of what she would do if she found it—but if nothing else, she needed to know where it was.

Jessica snapped on the light in her rcom and opened the door to the bathroom she and Elizabeth shared. Crossing in front of the sink, she opened her twin's door a crack.

Elizabeth was in bed, asleep.

Jessica opened the door a bit wider. "The mask, the mask," she muttered to herself. Luckily, it wasn't on Elizabeth's face.

Jessica studied her sleeping sister's expression. *Corrina's sister does look like you,* she thought. Then she sighed. *Which doesn't help me find the mask.*

On tiptoe, Jessica walked over to Elizabeth's chest of drawers. But before she reached it, she saw something that made her gasp.

A corner of the mask was sticking out from under Elizabeth's pillow.

Quickly, Jessica went to Elizabeth's bedside. She touched the rubbery material of the mask with one hand. *Ugh.* Shutting her eyes tight, she pulled as hard as she could.

But when she did, Elizabeth muttered in her sleep and grabbed her pillow tighter. Though the mask stretched, it didn't move. With a sigh, Jessica let go and waited for Elizabeth to relax her grip.

"Turn over, Elizabeth," she whispered, praying her sister would somehow pick up the message.

Elizabeth murmured something and clutched the pillow tighter.

"What was that?" Jessica leaned closer.

Elizabeth repeated it. Jessica thought it sounded a little like "The moon, the moon."

That did it. Jessica *had* to get the mask away from her sister. With one hand, Jessica picked up Elizabeth's wrist and tried to lift it off the pillow. She was ready to pull the mask out with the other hand before Elizabeth could wake up, but she couldn't pry Elizabeth's hand from the pillow. She seemed to be holding on with all her might.

Elizabeth murmured more loudly, and this time Jessica understood her words perfectly. "The moon, the moon," Elizabeth wailed, frowning in her sleep. She was clutching the pillow more tightly than ever.

Jessica backed away. It was obvious that her twin wouldn't let her have the mask just like that. Elizabeth seemed to be guarding that mask with her life.

Twelve

That night Jessica dreamed she was in Corrina Black's house and there were moons everywhere. Huge orange full moons, little tiny yellow crescents, moons hanging from the ceiling, moons bolted to the floor. As for Corrina, she was nowhere in sight.

Jessica stumbled among the moons, looking for something. But she couldn't figure out what. Whatever it was, it wasn't on Corrina's table, and it wasn't on the shelves. Then Jessica looked up at the portraits and gasped. The painting of Corrina as a young girl was gone—and Corrina herself was standing inside the frame. Her eyes stared out at Jessica with an expression of terrible sadness.

Jessica turned away from the awful sight and faced the portrait of Corrina's sister. To Jessica's horror, the girl in the portrait was changing—the blond hair was pulled back into a ponytail, the face narrowed slightly, and a dimple appeared in her cheek. Jessica recognized the girl in the portrait, all right. She was Elizabeth.

Jessica couldn't tear her eyes away. The painting of Elizabeth seemed to spring to life before her eyes. The eyes screwed up, and a single tear began to drop down Elizabeth's face.

Suddenly Elizabeth began to cry out, in the saddest voice Jessica had ever heard. "Oh, Jess, oh, Jess, help me. . . ."

Wait a minute. Jessica sat bolt upright in bed and switched on the light. She wasn't dreaming—Elizabeth really was calling her name!

"Jess, oh, Jessica!" Elizabeth was standing over Jessica's bed. Her eyes were red, as if she'd been crying.

"Elizabeth!" Jessica gasped. "What's wrong?" She reached out for her sister's hand.

"I—I don't exactly know," Elizabeth began exhaustedly. "I just feel—all weird."

"Weird how?" Automatically Jessica reached for her sister's hand. She wanted to ask Elizabeth about the mask, but she was afraid to. "Tell me."

"It's not that I'm sick or anything," Elizabeth told her. "At least, I don't think so." She shook her head and sat down, leaning up against Jessica. "It's just—

strange. Like everything is changing somehow."

It is, it is! Jessica wanted to cry out. Instead, she wrapped her arms tightly around her sister. "It'll be OK," she said soothingly, rocking her twin back and forth. "Things'll be fine. I promise."

"I hope you're right," Elizabeth said sleepily.

"Of course I'm right," Jessica assured her. *I'm just glad you're here and not in your room with that mask.*

Suddenly, Jessica's eyes lit up. *That's right,* she thought. *Elizabeth's not clutching the mask right now. In fact, she's probably too tired to even think about the mask. Now's the perfect time for me to grab it.*

"Why don't I help you back into bed again," Jessica suggested, rubbing her sister's back. "I'll tuck you back in, and—everything will be just fine."

Elizabeth broke away. "Thanks, but no thanks," she said, her eyes narrowing. "Don't bother. I'll be OK. You just go back to sleep." She stood up quickly, and darted back to her own bedroom.

Jessica settled back into her bed, an icy finger of fear stealing over her heart. It's like—like the mask's already taking over.

"See, the moon is always turning as it revolves," Steven explained at breakfast the next morning. He picked up an apple and moved it through the air.

"So there's a side that's always facing away from us, understand?"

"No," Jessica said, frowning. "And I'm trying to eat my breakfast. Do you mind?" She took a spoonful of cereal.

Steven glared at her. "How about you, Mom?" he demanded. "Did you catch what I was saying?"

Mrs. Wakefield glanced up from the newspaper she was reading. "Sorry, Steven, I wasn't listening," she said. "Was it about astronomy again?"

"Uh-huh," Steven said happily. He picked the apple back up. "See, the moon is always—"

"Actually, Steven, why don't you tell me later?" Mrs. Wakefield looked at her watch and set her coffee cup down hastily. "I have an important meeting this morning, and I should get ready."

Steven sighed, irritated, as his mother left the kitchen. How could anybody choose a meeting over astronomy?

Just then, Steven heard Elizabeth coming down the stairs. *Funny how late she's been sleeping these days*, he thought. He brightened as she came into the kitchen. "Hey, Elizabeth!" he greeted her. "Want to see something neat?"

"No possible way," Elizabeth snarled. She went to the pantry and started dumping cereal boxes onto the floor.

Steven stared at his sister. She was getting

weirder and weirder. Dumping cereal boxes on the floor? Not even Jessica did that!

Jessica was staring at Elizabeth, too, her brow furrowed. "I'm glad you're not wearing that mask, Elizabeth. I hope you—"

"Get out of my life, loser," Elizabeth snapped, tearing open a box of cereal and pouring it into her bowl till it overflowed.

"Whoa! You're making kind of a mess," Steven pointed out.

"Sor-ry," Elizabeth said, not making a move to clean it up.

Steven stole a look at Jessica. She looked as though she'd just been slapped. He looked back to Elizabeth and swallowed hard. Something was wrong, all right.

"Hey, what's eating *you?*" he asked jokingly, hoping to tease her out of her mood. "You should be psyched—only three more days till Halloween." He poured himself a second glass of milk.

"Oh, I'm psyched, all right," Elizabeth agreed, a glint in her eye. "I'm *real* psyched." She fixed Jessica with a look—and then she laughed.

Steven winced. He'd never heard Elizabeth laugh like that before—it felt like spiders crawling down his backbone. He realized he'd heard a laugh a lot like that somewhere before. It belonged to a mean girl in his sisters' grade. "You know, you sound a lot like Betsy Martin," Steven told her.

Elizabeth's face hardened. "You better not say anything against Betsy," she warned, her voice low. "Nothing, understand?" She drew her finger quickly across her throat. Then, without a word, she grabbed her backpack and flounced out the door.

"Whew!" Steven whistled. "You sure scare me, sister dear!" He turned to Jessica. "What's gotten into her, anyway? She's acting even weirder than *you*."

Jessica shook her head and stared down at her bowl of cereal.

Great, Steven thought with a snort. *They're both totally bonkers. Sisters!*

Steven checked over his homework for astronomy class. *Let's see, today the moon should rise at—*

"Steven?"

Steven looked up. Jessica was standing over him, a worried expression on her face. "Steven, I just wanted to know—" She wiped her forehead. "What time does the moon rise today?"

"The moon?" Steven repeated. *What do you know? Someone around here appreciates my vast knowledge!*

"Yes, the moon," Jessica told him timidly. "Can you find out?"

"No problemo," Steven assured her importantly.

He ran his finger down his homework chart. "There, see? A little after four."

"A little after four," Jessica repeated, as if trying to cram it into her memory. "Thanks!"

"You're welcome," Steven began, but Jessica was already out the door. With a sigh, he went back to his chart and his third glass of milk.

Sisters!

"If this is really cake, then I'm a frog," Amy Sutton announced to Maria Slater at lunchtime.

Maria grinned. She took a bite of her own slice and chewed. "Hmm. I see what you mean."

"I think it's flavored rubber," Amy said, dropping her fork back onto her plate. She looked over her shoulder. "I wonder where Elizabeth is."

Maria cleared her throat and leaned forward. "Actually, speaking of Elizabeth, something's going on, Amy. I wish I knew what." Quickly she filled Amy in on her phone call to the Wakefields' yesterday.

Amy raised her eyebrows. "Do you think Jessica's playing tricks again?"

"I wish I could say yes, but I'm really not so sure," Maria admitted. "I mean, why would Jessica keep on doing this? It's not like her."

"It's not like Elizabeth, either," Amy pointed out. "It's a lot less like Elizabeth, if you ask me."

"I know, but—" Maria began. "There she is," she

said, interrupting herself. "Hey, Elizabeth!" She waved.

"Hi, Elizabeth," Amy added, moving over to make room.

Elizabeth walked past the table without stopping, her tray loaded down with five pieces of cake. "Who needs this bunch of goody-goodies?" she snarled. Their mouths wide open, Maria and Amy watched Elizabeth head for Betsy Martin's table and sit down.

"OK, now I know for sure—no way is that Elizabeth," Maria said firmly. "It's got to be Jessica." She started up from the table. "Let's go over there and tell her what a jerk she's being."

"OK." Amy sounded doubtful. "But doesn't Jessica usually sit with the other Unicorns?" She gazed down to where Elizabeth was sitting. "I mean, Betsy Martin?"

Maria frowned. "It's Jessica," she said as firmly as she could manage. "If it isn't, then *I'm* the one who's a frog." She hurried across the cafeteria to Betsy's table.

"Amy and I are sick and tired of your games, Jessica," she said sternly. "Please stop them right now!"

Elizabeth stared, contempt all over her face. "You think I'm Jessica?" she said with a sneer. "That little twerp?"

"Who invited these clowns, huh?" Betsy Martin asked.

"Not me," Elizabeth said, pretending to hold her nose. She laughed. "Clear out, you two," she ordered. She jerked her thumb over to the Unicorn table. "If you want Jessica, look for her with the other babies who play clubhouse."

Maria glanced at the Unicorner. *Oh, no.* There was Jessica, all right. Unmistakably Jessica, sitting between Lila and Ellen. Jessica, staring over at them sadly and shaking her head.

That's Jessica, this is Elizabeth, and I'm a frog. Maria looked down at the floor. She felt like crying. "Ribbit," she muttered.

It was one of the worst days of Jessica's life. All day long, from every direction, she heard the same sets of words, over and over again. "You need to have a talk with your sister." "Hey, Jessica, what's wrong with Elizabeth today?" "Why is your sister so rude?"

It's not just one or two people, either, Jessica thought gloomily, grabbing her books as the last bell rang. *It's everybody!*

Todd Wilkins, Elizabeth's sort-of boyfriend, stopped her as she came into the hall. "Jessica, maybe you can tell me—is something bothering Elizabeth?" he asked.

He looks terrible, Jessica thought with a rush of pity. She sighed. "Whatever it is, it's not your fault, Todd—OK?" she told him firmly.

Todd rubbed his cheeks. "I guess. I wanted to go trick-or-treating with her, but now—" He shook his head.

"I'm sure it will all work out," Jessica lied, moving on to find Elizabeth. She hadn't gone three feet before Mr. Bowman, the twins' English teacher, approached her.

"Jessica. Just the person I wanted to see. Can you tell me what's wrong with your sister?" he asked, a frown covering his face.

"No, Mr. Bowman." Jessica shook her head. "I'm sorry, I can't." *And if I could, you wouldn't believe me,* she added to herself, dashing off.

Janet Howell caught up with Jessica just as she escaped from Mr. Bowman. "You wouldn't believe what that sister of yours just said to me, Jessica," she said, her eyes blazing.

Jessica suspected that she would too believe it. "I'm sorry, Janet," she mumbled.

"You'd better be." Janet folded her arms and stared hard at Jessica. "You really should do something about her, you know."

Jessica nodded unhappily. *Janet's right,* she thought. *I should.*

But what?

Jessica checked her watch. Two minutes to four o'clock. *If this is the worst day of my life,* she thought miserably, *then this is the worst hour of the worst day of my life.*

Ever since school had let out, Jessica had been following Elizabeth around. She couldn't forget what Corrina had told her. "Watch the rising of the moon," she repeated softly. According to Steven, moonrise was in just a few minutes, and Jessica had to make sure Elizabeth didn't have that mask on when the moon rose or else—

Jessica swallowed. She didn't want to think about the "or else."

"Oink, oink, oink!" Betsy Martin called to her. Elizabeth and her new friends were walking arm in arm up and down the sidewalk near Casey's ice cream parlor, taking up as much of the sidewalk as they could. When people came in the other direction, they didn't step aside. Instead they forced the other people to walk into the street. *Some game,* Jessica thought bitterly.

Elizabeth even looked different, Jessica realized, staring at the old clothes her sister was wearing. Nothing matched, nothing fit right. There were even big holes in Elizabeth's sweatshirt. *She's never been much for fashion,* Jessica thought, *but this is ridiculous!*

"Oink, oink!" Betsy hollered again.

Elizabeth turned back to look at Jessica. "She's so fat, no one could walk around *her* and stay on the sidewalk!" she jeered. Jessica bit her lip. *I must not, must not lose my temper,* she warned herself.

At least the mask wasn't anywhere in sight.

The group approached an old man waiting for the bus. As Jessica watched, Betsy and three other kids began walking clockwise around the man. At the same time, Elizabeth led the rest of the kids around him from the other direction. Each time they passed by they tightened the circle.

"What are you kids doing?" the old man cried, looking alarmed.

"We're waiting for the bus!" Elizabeth said, with a snicker. She pretended to grab for the man's nose, while Betsy laughed hysterically.

Jessica couldn't stand it any longer. "Will you quit it!" she burst out, coming forward and pushing Elizabeth out of the way. "Haven't you done enough mean things for one day?"

"Well, if it isn't Little Miss Goody Two-Shoes!" Elizabeth mocked her. "Why don't you go help your paper dolls across the street, huh?"

"Elizabeth Wakefield!" Jessica shouted.

"'Elizabeth Wakefield!'" Elizabeth mimicked, placing her hands prissily on her hips.

Betsy and her friends laughed again, but Jessica wasn't paying attention. Instead, she was watching the glow that appeared in the sky over her sister's left shoulder. Jessica felt her muscles relax. It was the moon peeking over the horizon. She'd never seen it so large. Or so red.

Still, it was up. And Elizabeth hadn't been wearing the mask when it rose. Jessica breathed a sigh of relief and turned her back on her sister, who was still laughing wickedly.

But Corrina was right, she realized sadly as she walked back toward her house. *The mask is beginning to work even when Elizabeth isn't wearing it!*

Thirteen

"Corrina?"

It was eight o'clock on Tuesday evening, and Jessica had told her parents she was going to Lila's. Really, though, she wanted to talk to Corrina about what had happened that afternoon. She peered through the window of the old Luna place and tapped on the glass. "Corrina?" she called again, a little more loudly this time.

There was no answer.

"I guess I'll try the door," Jessica muttered, crossing the yard to the doorway she'd gone through yesterday. She reached out her hand—and gasped.

The wall in front of her was completely solid.

I could have sworn there was a door here, Jessica said to herself. Gently she touched where she was sure the door had been. It felt just the same as every other section of the rundown wall. The paint was peeling, the wood rotted in places.

"I guess I was wrong," Jessica said softly, staring up and down the wall to see if there was a door somewhere else. There wasn't. So how was she supposed to get in? How did Corrina come in and out?

Frowning, Jessica knocked on the wall, right where the door would have been if there had been a door. She waited, but there was still no answer.

Well, if she's not home, then she's not home, Jessica thought at last. She turned and started walking slowly through the tall grass toward the fence. She was about to slip back through the bars when she heard a voice on the sidewalk.

"Happy Halloween, everybody!"

An egg soared through the air toward the old Luna place. Jessica whirled around in time to see it smash against the crescent window in the attic. Pieces of shell flew everywhere, and the yolk slid stickily down the glass. "Nice shot!" somebody else yelled. Jessica froze. _Betsy Martin's voice._

Jessica crouched down. Betsy came into view, laughing loudly. She held what looked like a can of shaving cream. Behind her came three of her friends and—Elizabeth.

Jessica's heart sank as Elizabeth let fly with an egg of her own. It crashed into the windshield of a pickup truck parked on the street.

"Bull's-eye!" Betsy shouted raucously. The others laughed.

"Hey, let's knock this over!" Elizabeth suggested, her eye falling on Corrina's rickety fence.

"The witch's fence? All right!" Betsy shook the rusty old fence, and Elizabeth and a few of the other kids joined in.

"Take that, witch lady!" Elizabeth sang out.

Stop, stop, Jessica pleaded, holding her breath.

A door slammed across the street. "Beat it, kids!" A neighbor had come out onto her front porch. "Go bug somebody else."

Elizabeth laughed maniacally. Running into the road, she threw a roll of toilet paper up into the woman's front yard. The roll unwound in the air, draped itself over several branches of a big oak tree, and plonked down on the roof of the woman's car.

"Get out of here, you hooligans!" the woman shouted.

"Takes one to know one!" Elizabeth snapped back in the sassiest voice Jessica had ever heard.

Jessica couldn't stand it any longer. She squeezed through the fence and started running for home.

But as she reached her own front porch, Jessica had to stop running. Her body was racked with sobs.

I always thought Betsy Martin was the meanest

person in the world, she thought, crying harder. *But now I have to admit it—*

Elizabeth's become even meaner than she is!

"Mrs. Irene Nicholas," said the sign on the door in front of Steven. "Chairperson, Sweet Valley High School Science Department."

Steven read the sign again. *I hope she won't think this is just a stupid question*, he said to himself. With teachers, you never could tell.

He took a deep breath and knocked.

A large woman with glasses opened the door. "Oh, hello, Steven," she said warmly. "My prize astronomy pupil. Come in. Have a seat. If you can find one."

Your prize astronomy pupil? Steven thought, flabbergasted. He looked around Mrs. Nicholas's office—and was even more flabbergasted than before.

The floor was knee-deep in scientific equipment. Microscopes and test-tube racks hung off the shelves. Science textbooks filled every inch of Mrs. Nicholas's desk. Astronomy posters were tacked all over the walls. *It's a federal disaster area*, Steven thought, wrinkling up his nose. *It's even worse than Jessica's room!*

Steven decided to remain standing. "Um—I just had a question, Mrs. Nicholas," he said shyly.

"A question?" Mrs. Nicholas perched on top of a pile of science magazines. "Sure. Shoot!"

Steven cleared his throat. "Well, it might be kind of a stupid question."

Mrs. Nicholas made a harrumphing sound. "The only stupid question, Steven, is the one—"

"—the one you don't ask," Steven finished. "I know, I know." He'd heard that line often enough. Did teachers really believe it, or was that just something they liked to say? "Anyway, what I wanted to know is—is it possible for the moon to be bright red when it rises?"

Mrs. Nicholas took off her glasses and wiped them on her sleeve. "Bright red? The moon is always a little reddish—more like an orange color— when it first rises, because we're looking at it through more atmosphere than when it's higher in the sky. But bright red sounds unlikely. Why?"

Because I've seen it two days in a row now, Steven thought. But he decided to hold off on mentioning that for now. "Just curious."

Mrs. Nicholas put her glasses back on. "A very big forest fire could put enough red light in the sky to make the moon seem a little red itself," she told Steven. "I suppose that if the sun's rays were to bend in an unexpected way, that could create a bit of redness, too."

"A bit of redness?" Steven repeated. "How

about a real fiery red? You know, a"—he hesitated—"a blood red?"

Mrs. Nicholas laughed. "No."

"Definitely not?" Steven leaned forward. "What
if someone told you they'd seen the moon rise all
blood red?"

"Then I'd say they were seeing things," Mrs.
Nicholas replied. "Trust me. It can't happen."

Steven bit his lip. "OK. Thanks." He darted out
of his teacher's office. *But I know I really saw it,* he
told himself. *And it wasn't just me, either. Jessica saw
it, too!*

Didn't she?

Steven rubbed his eyes. Maybe he'd been peer-
ing through that little telescope too much. He made
a mental note to ask Jessica a question or two when
he got home from school.

Jessica walked home from school Wednesday
afternoon, keeping an eye out for Elizabeth.
*Moonrise isn't till almost five, so I still have time to look
for her.*

She knew that the mask had already begun to
take over, but she pushed the thought out of her
mind. *There's still time, there's still time,* she chanted
silently.

Jessica walked on, lost in thought. Soon she
reached Corrina's fence. *Maybe Corrina's home now,*

she said to herself, squeezing through the fence, which felt even looser than usual.

Jessica went to the window and stopped short. *The door was back.*

"This is totally ridiculous," Jessica muttered. "First it's here, then it's gone, now it's back. Who is Corrina, anyway—Harry Houdini or somebody?" She banged on the door as hard as she could, half afraid that it would disappear again before Corrina could hear her. "Corrina!" she shouted. "Corrina! It's me, Jessica!"

All at once the door stood wide open. "I heard you the first time," Corrina said, smiling. As she led Jessica to the old sofa in the living room, Jessica rubbed her eyes. It looked as though Corrina's crescent moon had winked at her! *This is just getting weirder all the time*, she thought.

"I'm sorry I wasn't here yesterday," Corrina was saying softly.

Jessica blinked. "How did you know—?"

"Tell me," Corrina cut in. "Has the problem gotten worse?"

Jessica looked down at the floor. "Yes, Corrina," she said. "It seems like the mask is—like it's starting to take over."

"I see." Corrina sat in silence for a moment. "Does your sister have the mask now? Do you know where it is?"

"No." Jessica thought hard. "It might be in her room. But I don't know for sure."

Corrina got up and began to pace around the room. "Did she wear it during moonrise yesterday?"

Jessica shook her head vigorously. "No. I made sure." Then she buried her face in her hands. "Oh, Corrina, isn't there anything we can do?" she sobbed.

Corrina touched Jessica's arm, and Jessica looked up. "Let me think," she said. She stared up at the portraits above the mantelpiece.

Jessica waited as long as she could stand. "Please, Corrina, please," she burst out at last. "If you can't help me, I don't know what I'm going to do, I really don't! You're the only one who can save Elizabeth!"

"No." Corrina set her jaw. "There you are wrong." She rushed to the bookshelves and plucked a book from the middle of a pile. "I've just gotten an idea," she said, turning the pages quickly. She stopped and held out a warning finger to Jessica. "But understand, my dear—Elizabeth is the only one who can save herself."

Jessica's face fell. "How?"

Corrina brushed a strand of her hair out of her eyes. "According to this book, there is one chance for your sister."

"What's that?" Jessica whispered hoarsely.

Corrina consulted the book. "Your sister must destroy the mask during a lunar eclipse," she said. "This, and only this, can destroy the curse."

What? Jessica stared at Corrina with bewilderment. "But—but—but that's not possible," she stammered.

"It is the only way." Corrina shut the book, releasing a cloud of dust, and set it back in its place.

"How can I get Elizabeth to destroy the mask?" Jessica asked, her voice rising in pitch. "I can't even get her to take it out from under her pillow! And during an eclipse? You might as well tell me she has to throw it up to the moon!" She bit her lip to keep from crying.

"I am sorry." Corrina seemed lost in thought again. Once more she stared up at the portraits.

Suddenly Jessica had an idea. *Of course!* "I know!" She stood up excitedly. "I look just like her. I'll find the mask—and destroy it myself!"

Corrina shook her head firmly. Jessica seemed to feel a chilly wind blowing directly from the crescent moon. "No," Corrina said. "The one who is cursed must remove the curse herself."

"That's not fair," Jessica said, folding her arms angrily. "Can't you do better than that? There must be something else."

"There is nothing else." Her voice sounded

tired. Jessica realized that Corrina's eyes had lost their sparkle. "I know how you must feel, Jessica."

No you don't, Jessica was ready to retort, but she stopped herself. "What if—what if I can't get Elizabeth to destroy the mask?" she asked nervously.

"Then the curse will continue to grow," Corrina replied. "Your sister will become more and more evil."

"How can she be more evil than she already is?" Jessica demanded.

Corrina's voice dropped to a whisper, and wind from the crescent seemed to grow colder than ever. "Do not say that, Jessica. There is real danger here. The curse does not stop with foolish Halloween pranks." She paused and stared hard at Jessica. "Even you, my dear. Even you are not safe."

"What do you mean?" Jessica asked, her voice squeaky in the dim room. She sat back down slowly.

Corrina sighed and looked above the mantelpiece. "The last girl who was cursed by that mask burned down her own house," she said slowly.

Jessica gasped. She felt sick to her stomach.

"Every member of her family perished in that fire," Corrina went on, as though talking to herself. "All but one."

Jessica leaned forward, her fingers digging into her palms. "Who—who was that?"

As Corrina opened her mouth to speak, Jessica saw the blood-red moon rising through the window across the room.

"Me," Corrina said quietly.

Fourteen

"What's that you're singing, Dad?" Steven asked after dinner on Wednesday night. He was studying his star charts at the kitchen table while his father wiped the counters.

"Singing?" Mr. Wakefield put down the cloth and stared blankly at his son. "Was I singing?"

Steven frowned. "Uh-huh." *Your voice could use some work,* he thought, but he was careful not to say it out loud.

"You were, Dad," Jessica chimed in. Her math book was open in front of her, but she didn't seem to be looking at it. "Something about—the moon, I think."

"Oh, that!" Mr. Wakefield laughed. "It's an old Irish folk song. 'For the rising of the moon,'" he warbled, "'for the rising of the moon! The pipes must play together for the rising of the moon.' That one?"

"Yeah, that one," Jessica said, nibbling her fingernails. `

"I don't think I've ever heard you sing it before," Steven said slowly. *The rising of the moon*, Steven thought, feeling a shiver beginning to creep along his back. *The rising of the moon?* He shut his eyes, and the image of a blood-red moon sprang into his mind.

"Could you, maybe—sing something else?" Jessica's voice broke the stillness. Steven's eyes snapped open. He stared at her curiously. *She did see it, then,* he thought. *I wasn't just imagining it.*

"Well, sure, I guess so," Mr. Wakefield said uncertainly, picking up the dishrag again. "'Found a peanut, found a peanut . . .'"

"Dad!" Jessica exclaimed. Then she cleared her throat. "Have you noticed something—something odd about Elizabeth lately?"

Steven pricked up his ears.

"Different?" Mr. Wakefield frowned. "She's been a little irritable, sure."

"Are you talking about Elizabeth?" Mrs. Wakefield asked, coming into the kitchen with a magazine. "She's spending an awful lot of time with those new friends of hers, isn't she?"

"Friends!" Jessica burst. "How could you call those girls *friends*? If you knew how horrible Elizabeth is when she's with them—"

Mrs. Wakefield ruffled Jessica's hair. "If you

knew the number of times Elizabeth has said something like that about you and *your* friends—"

"But that's me!" Jessica protested. "Elizabeth is different! She's a nice person, and she's never *not* been a nice person—till now."

"She's just going through a phase," Mr. Wakefield said soothingly. "It's nothing to worry about."

Steven winced. He hated that expression. If his parents could be believed, he'd been through more phases than he could count.

He couldn't help wondering about Elizabeth. He didn't like to give Jessica credit for anything, but he had to admit, she had a point. Elizabeth wasn't acting like herself lately, that was for sure.

Jessica looked almost tearful. "And—and—that mask—"

"Yeah, it really isn't Elizabeth's kind of thing," Steven put in.

"Now, now." Mr. Wakefield gave the counter a final wipe and pitched the cloth into the sink. "Two points! Elizabeth's just developing different interests, that's all. People do that. Steven, you do it all the time."

"I do not!" Steven stared at his father, hands on his hips.

"Sure you do. What do you want to be when you grow up?" Mr. Wakefield challenged him.

"That's easy," Steven answered. "An astronomer."

"Exactly." Mr. Wakefield smiled. "Last month, if I remember correctly, you were all set to join the Chicago Bulls. Last summer, you were going to study dinosaurs. Then there were the times you wanted to be a marine biologist, an astronaut, a reporter, a fireman"—Mr. Wakefield started ticking them off on his fingers—"an FBI agent, a filmmaker— Have I forgotten anything?"

"Race car driver," Steven said automatically. "Sure I've wanted to be a bunch of stuff. But that's different." He waved his hand in the air. "See, what I *really* want to be is an astronomer. All the other things I don't care about all that much."

Mr. Wakefield just smiled.

"It *is* different, Dad," Jessica said earnestly. "Changing his mind is, like, part of Steven's personality. Elizabeth doesn't *ever* change. Don't you get it?"

"Right," Steven agreed. "She's out with Betsy Martin, isn't she? I'd say that's a pretty big change for my sister."

"Betsy Martin is *so* mean," Jessica said dramatically.

Mrs. Wakefield laughed and gave Jessica a hug. "You can't expect things to be the same forever," she said. "Children develop at different rates, that's all. Next week she'll probably move on to some other friend."

Great, Steven told himself. *Just what we need—a lecture on child psychology.*

Jessica stood up, clutching her math book. "Well, I'm going to go upstairs to study."

Her voice sounds higher than usual, Steven thought, watching her leave the room.

Obviously, something was really bugging her.

Jessica was sobbing into her pillow a few minutes later, when there was a knock at the door. "Who is it?" she called, hastily drying her eyes. *Maybe it's Elizabeth*, she told herself, *and everything will be all right* after all. . . .

Yeah, sure. And maybe I'll be lead vocalist on Johnny Buck's next album.

"It's me." Steven's voice came through the door. "Can I come in for a minute?"

Steven? Jessica blew her nose and opened the door a crack. "What do you want?" she demanded, sounding more cross than she intended.

"Hey, don't bite my head off!" Steven said, shoving the door the rest of the way open. He came in and perched at the end of Jessica's bed. "It's not *my* fault."

"No," Jessica agreed. She felt too tired to argue, and anyway she knew Steven was right. "Listen, Steven, what do you want? I'm supposed to be studying and—"

"I just wanted to ask you something," Steven said, interrupting. "You told me that you'd seen the moon rise all bloody red, right?"

Jessica suddenly felt all creepy again. She nodded slowly. "Right."

Steven ran his hand through his hair. He took a deep breath. "And, well, I was just wondering. Did you see it again today?"

Without warning, a picture leaped into Jessica's mind: the moon rising outside Corrina's window. Her skin prickled. "Yeah, I did," she said in a half whisper.

Steven frowned. "So did I. It was bloodier than ever today." He shuddered slightly, as if remembering what he'd seen. "I saw it rising just as Elizabeth came up the stairs this afternoon."

Jessica's heart went cold. "Elizabeth? Was she wearing that mask?"

Steven shook his head. "Why do you ask?"

Jessica hesitated. "Steven," she said, sitting up and narrowing her eyes, "you agree with me that Elizabeth's acting weird, right?"

Steven folded his arms. "Well, I don't know if I'd say 'weird,' exactly. I mean, there's 'weird' and then there's—"

"Oh, spare me!" Jessica burst out. "Just say it."

For a moment Steven looked stricken. Then he sighed. "Oh, OK. She's been acting weird."

"All right." Jessica came to a decision. "I'm going to tell you something that's going to sound completely unbelievable. OK?"

Steven raised an eyebrow and nodded.

"But you have to believe it," Jessica went on. "Because—"

"Because why?"

Jessica stared straight at her brother. "Because every single word of it is true."

"So let me get this straight," Steven said ten minutes later. "The witch who lives at the old Luna place gave you a bottle of something she said was iced tea—and you actually *drank* it?"

Jessica sighed impatiently. "That's not the point, Steven, and you know it. The question is, do you believe me or not? Because if you don't, you can get out of my room right this minute." She put on her fiercest look and began to stand up.

"All right, already, I believe!" Steven said quickly.

"That's better." Jessica flopped back on the bed. She wasn't at all sure that Steven really did believe her story, but she decided it didn't matter. *Even if he thinks it's just a big joke,* she thought, *maybe he can help me anyway.* "So when's the next lunar eclipse?" she asked.

Steven hooted. "Don't you remember? I told you all about it a few days ago."

"Well, I wasn't listening," Jessica retorted. *Give me a break!* she felt like saying. *Why does he think I should pay attention to everything he says?* "So just tell me when it is."

"Day after tomorrow," Steven said. "Halloween night. At midnight."

Halloween night? Jessica sat straight up. "Then we've got our work cut out for us."

"How's that?" Steven looked puzzled.

"Elizabeth's got to destroy that mask during a lunar eclipse," Jessica reminded him. "Which means that we've got to stick with her on Halloween—somehow. Which doesn't give us much time to plan." Her mind raced. "Maybe—maybe I could ask her to dress up as a two-headed sea monster with me." Jessica got up and began to pace. "I told her that was a kind of a stupid idea, but I could say I've changed my mind. Yeah, maybe—"

"Wait a second, Jessica," Steven broke in. "From what you're telling me, it doesn't sound like she'd go for that idea right now."

Jessica froze. "I guess you're right." She felt as though she'd been riding in a hot-air balloon that had just sprung a leak. She could hear Elizabeth's new voice in her mind: *"You want to do what? Of all the incredibly dumb, idiotic, three-year-old ideas . . . "* She grimaced. "It wouldn't work."

"Let me see," Steven said thoughtfully. "If the eclipse starts at midnight . . . Did the cat woman down at the Luna place say Elizabeth had to destroy the mask during the eclipse, or only during that night?"

"You mean Corrina." Jessica thought back. "During the eclipse."

"That makes it tough," Steven said, scratching his ear. Suddenly his face lit up. "I think I have an idea," he told Jessica.

"What is it?" Jessica leaned forward with excitement.

Steven chuckled. "Patience, patience!" he told her. "Didn't you ever hear that curiosity killed the cat?"

"If you don't tell me right this instant," Jessica demanded, "curiosity's going to end up killing you." She grabbed his right arm and pinned it behind his back.

"All right!" Steven said quickly. "Here's my plan." As he described it, Jessica listened with growing excitement.

It just might work, she realized when he had finished. *It just might work!*

When the final bell rang on Thursday afternoon, Jessica quickly slipped into the girls' room to change her clothes. Instead of books, her backpack was full of the ugliest, most beat-up clothes in her closet: torn blue jeans, a T-shirt that had never fit, a moth-eaten sweater that hadn't been washed in months. *Ugh, gross*, Jessica thought, but she put the clothes on anyway. Then she stood back to examine herself in the mirror. Just to be safe, she mussed up her hair a little.

The door swung open and Amy came into the bathroom. "Oh—hi, Elizabeth," she said with a gulp, crossing to the sink as far across the room from Jessica as possible.

It's working, Jessica thought excitedly. She put on her best evil Elizabeth face. "Will you just quit following me around?" she snarled.

Amy jumped. "Um, I'm—I'm not—" she stammered.

Jessica groaned inwardly. Even though she knew it was all in a good cause, Jessica felt a surge of sympathy for Amy. It must be awful to have your best friend turn on you without your knowing why. Afraid to say anything else, Jessica headed into the hall, banging the door behind her.

"Now to find Betsy," she muttered, striding quickly through the halls. Usually it's really easy to pretend to be Elizabeth—all you have to do was act super nice. But today—

Today was a different story.

Betsy was standing on the front steps of the school. "Hey, Elizabeth!" Her eyes traveled up and down Jessica's outfit. "Real cool, kid. *Way*, way cool."

"Thanks." Jessica made her voice sound as tough as possible. "So there's a party on Courage Mountain tomorrow at midnight." She winked at Betsy, her heart beating furiously. "Let's crash it."

"You kidding, or what?" Betsy looked at Jessica's face.

"Uh-uh!" Jessica burst out. "Cross my heart and hope to— I mean, no way," she added, waving the idea away with her hand.

Betsy rolled her eyes. "Sometimes you're still such a dweeb," Then her eyes glinted. "So what party?"

"High school party," Jessica said, thrusting her chin forward the way she had seen a tough teenager do in a movie once. "You game? Or what?"

"Who told you?" Betsy sounded suspicious.

"My brother." *Which is the truth*, Jessica reminded herself—*for a change!* She moved closer to Betsy and winked. "So are you coming? Or are you chicken?"

"Ha!" Betsy made an ugly noise back in her throat. "Don't call *me* scared, sister. I'll be there—if it isn't past *your* bedtime!"

All right! Jessica thought. Stage One, complete. She felt like dancing. "Gotta go," she said, flashing Betsy a grin out of the corner of her mouth. "Catch you later."

"Yeah, later," Betsy began. "and hey—"

But Jessica was gone.

One more errand, Jessica thought.

She darted back inside the school building and

into the library. She dropped her backpack on one of the tables. "Be at the party," she wrote in cursive on a sheet of notebook paper. Then she hesitated.

No good. Elizabeth will recognize my writing.

Tearing off a new sheet of paper, Jessica began again. In plain block capitals, she wrote, "BE AT THE PARTY OR DIE." *That looks better.* Jessica held it in front of her and stared at it. Just to be on the safe side, she added the word "FOOL." "Be at the party or die, fool," she read quietly. *Sounds like Betsy, all right.*

Jessica sighed. *Now, how would Elizabeth know which party the note was talking about?* She drummed her fingers on the table and thought. *Aha!* She added another line. "THE COURAGE MOUNTAIN PARTY HALLOWEEN NIGHT. DUH!" *Better.* Next to that, she wrote the words "HIGH SCHOOL" and underlined them three times.

Jessica checked her work again and nodded. One more line. "P.S.," she read as she formed the letters. "MAKE SURE YOU BRING THAT AWESOMELY RE-VOLTING MASK."

No, wait a minute. Betsy's not a good speller, is she? Jessica carefully erased the "o" in awesomely and turned it into a "u." *Awesumely. That should do it.*

Jessica signed the note "Betsy M.," slid out of her seat, and headed for her sister's locker. Crossing her fingers, she dropped the note inside.

Fifteen

◇

"What wonderful costumes, girls," Mandy's mother said, filling Halloween bags with candy. It was Halloween night, and Jessica was out trick-or-treating with her Unicorn friends.

"Mine is a real figure-skating costume from the Olympics," Lila bragged, strutting a little. "Isn't it awesome?"

"It's beautiful," Mrs. Miller replied. "And Mary, I can't imagine how many hours you must have worked to put your outfit together."

"Thanks, Mrs. Miller," Mary said, touching her gypsy skirt and veil with pride.

Janet stepped forward. "What do you think, Mrs. Miller?" she asked, spinning around to show off her ball gown. "My mother knows the designer who makes all the clothes for the Queen of

England—well, not the queen, exactly, but one of her very best friends. Do you like it?"

"It's lovely," Mrs. Miller said appreciatively.

Jessica sighed impatiently. Watching her friends show off their Halloween costumes was about the last thing she wanted to do just then. Her own costume wasn't exactly anything to brag about. She'd been so worried about Elizabeth that she hadn't given her costume another thought till about five o'clock that day. At that point, all she could find was an old sheet.

Mrs. Miller peered off into the darkness. "Who's that down there at the bottom of the steps?"

"It's Jessica," Lila said immediately, rolling her eyes. "Some great costume *she's* got," she said.

"Totally original," Janet added dryly. "And I just bet it took loads and loads of time and money to put together."

"Why, I think it looks very nice," Mrs. Miller said, frowning at Janet. "Tell me, dear, what are you supposed to be?" she asked Jessica.

"With an old white sheet draped over her body?" Ellen sneered. "Can't you tell, Mrs. Miller? I thought it was obvious. She's a ghost, of course."

"Actually, I thought she was a peeled potato at first," Janet muttered to Lila in a voice loud enough for Jessica to hear. Jessica turned red. *It's a good thing the sheet covers my face*, she thought.

"Don't be silly," Lila said, reaching for the tag on Jessica's sheet. "See, it says "MACHINE WASH WARM." You wouldn't wash a potato in a washing machine, now would you?" She giggled hysterically.

Mrs. Miller sighed. "Have a good time trick-or-treating, girls," she said, closing the door gently but firmly.

"Whatever gave you the idea for such a stupid costume, anyway?" Lila demanded, as the group headed for the next house.

Jessica shrugged. She really didn't have the energy to get mad at Lila. "I thought it would be fun," she said simply.

"*Fun?*" Lila repeated incredulously. "What's fun about an old sheet?"

"You certainly aren't helping to let everybody know what good dressers the Unicorns are," Janet agreed, staring hard at Jessica.

"Really, Jessica," Tamara said. "Have you thought at all about the Unicorn image?"

But Jessica didn't say anything. She plodded on to the next house, checking her watch. Only eight o'clock. Another four hours before it was time to save Elizabeth.

Maria shook her head and sighed. "Doing a bicycle is fun, but I wish Elizabeth were here."

"I know what you mean," Amy told her. The

two girls were skating along in precise rhythm, connected by a cardboard frame. Each girl held a metal wheel in her hand. "It doesn't feel right, somehow."

Maria slowed down her strides. "There she is now."

"Where?" Amy peered off into the darkness.

"With Betsy Martin and her gang," Maria said sadly, hating the whole idea. As she watched, Elizabeth opened up a mailbox and shoved something inside. "What do you bet that's a rotten apple?" she asked, as Elizabeth ran off in a fit of giggles.

"Or worse." Amy shuddered. "Let's find out." Together they skated to the mailbox. Maria opened it gingerly and looked inside. "Ugh!" *How can Elizabeth do this?* she wondered. She pulled out the insides of a pumpkin. "Some great joke," she said bitterly.

"Hey, what's that?" Amy asked suddenly.

Two little girls were coming toward them. One was dressed as a ballerina, the other as a princess. The princess was in tears. "What's the matter, honey?" Maria called to her.

The girl only cried harder, but her friend spoke up. "A couple of big kids grabbed our candy bags." She looked as if she was about to cry herself.

Maria's heart sank. "Were they girls or boys?" she asked gently.

"Girls." The ballerina sniffed. "They just came

running down the sidewalk, and we couldn't stop them," she explained. "They yelled, 'Give us your candy!' and then they were gone before we could say anything."

"I'm so sorry," Maria said, giving the girls a hug. "Did—did one of them have long blond hair?" she asked, suspecting she already knew the answer.

"Uh-huh," the princess wailed. "And she had on an awful mask!"

"Do you know her?" the ballerina asked curiously. "Is she, like, one of your friends or something?"

"She used to be," Maria said sadly, catching Amy's eye. "But it seems like we don't really know her anymore."

"Hey, Jess!"

Normally Jessica's heart leaped when she saw Aaron Dallas, but not tonight. He was standing on the other side of the street, dressed in a basketball jersey and waving frantically to her. "Oh—hi, Aaron," she called back without enthusiasm.

"Happy Halloween!" Aaron called, starting across the road. "I've been looking all over for you."

"You have?" Letting the other Unicorns walk on, Jessica hung back to wait for Aaron. "How could you tell it was me?" she asked curiously.

"Oh, I'd know you anywhere," Aaron explained.

Jessica wasn't sure if that was a compliment or not, so she said nothing.

"What kind of a costume is that, anyway?" Aaron asked. "You're not a ghost, are you?" He looked at her, a frown spreading onto his face. "I mean, that would be kind of—well, not very original."

"Oh, I'm not a ghost," Jessica replied quickly. "I'm a mad scientist who's invented a formula that turns people evil."

"Oh." Aaron seemed doubtful. "And you spilled the formula all over yourself?"

Jessica felt a surge of irritation. "No, Aaron. I'm dressed this way to keep the bad guys from finding me."

"Uh-huh." Aaron scratched his head. "Why are the bad guys trying to find you if your formula makes people evil?"

Jessica sighed. "Never mind."

"Well, it doesn't matter anyway," Aaron decided. Shyly he reached out a hand and brushed it against her sheet. "It's a nice night," he said in a husky voice.

"Uh-huh." *He's trying to hold my hand,* Jessica realized. She thought back to just a few days ago, when she had been daydreaming about this exact thing happening. Somehow, she felt very differently about it today. With Elizabeth getting more evil all the time, she just didn't have the energy to think about holding hands with Aaron.

"And we're kind of alone." Aaron fumbled against the side of the sheet, searching for Jessica's hand.

Aaron really is pretty cute, Jessica reminded herself. Slowly she began to snake her own hand out of the sheet to meet his.

"We could—you know, trick-or-treat together for a while," Aaron suggested, sounding as though he'd just come up with the idea.

"That might be nice." Jessica's hand ran into a fold of the sheet. *No way out of here.* She reached further back and tried again.

"It really is a nice night." Aaron looked up at the sky. Jessica struggled to find a way to get her arm out. But whichever direction she pushed her hand, it kept getting stuck inside the sheet. She sighed impatiently.

"Are you all right, Jessica?" Aaron stepped closer and put his arm around her shoulders. "Look over there behind the buildings. Have you ever seen such a beautiful moon?"

Moon, Jessica thought. Suddenly she was in a panic. *The moon!* She didn't dare look at it. *In less than four hours*, she told herself, *there is going to be an eclipse, and if I can't find Elizabeth and figure out some way to get Elizabeth to destroy that mask, then—*

"Aaron, how often does a lunar eclipse come around?" Jessica demanded suddenly, twisting out of his reach.

Aaron looked surprised. "Gee, I don't have a clue, Jessica," he answered. He stepped forward again. "Why don't we just—"

But Jessica could listen no more. "I'm sorry, Aaron," she told him. A vision of Elizabeth had sprung into her mind—Elizabeth, looking more and more like Corrina's sister, a strange fiery glow surrounding her face. "I've got to go." She backed away. "I'll—I'll see you around. Or something." She shut her eyes. The image vanished. "Bye!"

"Hey, wait!" Aaron called. But it was too late. Jessica was out of sight.

At eleven o'clock, Jessica finished arranging the pillows under the covers on her bed. Stepping back, she examined her work. *Hmm. Not bad.* She nodded slowly. If you didn't look too closely, you might actually think a girl was sleeping in that bed.

Jessica drew a deep breath. *This has to work,* she promised herself, wishing she could believe it. *It has to!* Softly she came downstairs and crouched in the hall outside the living room.

"Well, I'm heading to that party now," she heard Steven say.

"What party?" Mrs. Wakefield sounded doubtful.

"You remember. The party on Courage Mountain," Steven reminded her. "I told you about it last week."

Jessica held her breath as she waited for her mother's answer.

"Well, it *is* Halloween," Mrs. Wakefield said at last, with a yawn. "Just don't be too late. By the way, where are the girls?"

"Jessica's asleep in bed," Steven assured her. "And Elizabeth will be home later—I guess."

"All right," Mrs. Wakefield agreed. "Have fun."

Steven came clumping through the kitchen and into the hall. "Get going!" he hissed at Jessica when he saw her. Quickly, Jessica stood up and followed her brother out to the garage. "I hope this works," he muttered to no one in particular, wheeling his bicycle into the driveway. Jessica said nothing. She hopped aboard her own bike and started to pedal furiously toward Courage Mountain.

"Hey!" Steven snapped from behind her. "Wait for me!"

But Jessica pedaled as fast as ever. Every minute counted. The cool night air seemed alive. *Hurry, hurry!* it urged her. She had to reach Courage Mountain before it was too late.

What if Elizabeth isn't there? she thought fearfully, and then she pushed the idea out of her mind. *She'll be there, she'll be there, she'll be there*, Jessica chanted silently.

Rounding a sharp curve a few blocks from home, Jessica began to pedal up Courage

Mountain. The going was harder now. Her breath came in short gasps, but she didn't dare slow her pace. Downshifting, she looked up and saw the outline of an old dead tree, its branches silhouetted eerily against—the moon.

The full moon, Jessica thought uneasily. She had never seen the moon look so enormous and so red.

"What a stupid pumpkin!" Betsy Martin sang out, staring at the Wakefields' porch rail.

Elizabeth laughed. She had been laughing all night, it seemed. She had laughed when Betsy had grabbed extra candy from the little kid who was passing out the treats at one house. She had laughed when the gang had grabbed a fourth-grader's hat, filled it with shaving cream, and shoved it back onto his head. She had laughed when Betsy had put rotten eggs behind the wheels of a parked car. She had even laughed when Betsy had placed a sign in front of the old Luna place that said "Just break the windoes if I don't here you ring the bell."

It's not trick-or-treat, she thought gleefully. *It's trick-or-trick, and boy, is it ever fun.*

Betsy's eyes roved up and down the gang behind her and came to rest on Elizabeth. "Smash it," she ordered. "Then we'll go crash the party you told us about."

I didn't tell you about that party, Elizabeth thought,

confused. *You were the one who told me.* "Did you say smash it?" she asked, a little uncertainly.

"What are you, stupid?" Some of the other kids laughed.

Elizabeth stared at Jessica's pumpkin. The candle flickered in the breeze. "Um—" she began.

"Oh, come on, don't be such a baby," Betsy said contemptuously.

Something deep inside Elizabeth was trying to send her a message, but Elizabeth did her best to ignore it. "Who are you calling a baby?" she demanded, marching across the lawn to the porch rail. She stared at Jessica's pumpkin. Then she hesitated.

"Buck, buck, buck!" Betsy taunted her.

Elizabeth slowly hefted the jack-o'-lantern in her hands.

"Just smash it." Betsy's voice grew menacing. "Smash it!"

"Go for it, Elizabeth!" someone shouted. "We'll be late for the party!"

Elizabeth looked at the windows of the darkened house. *They're all asleep in there,* she told herself with sudden certainty. *They'll never know.* Behind her mask she steeled herself to smash Jessica's pumpkin. Standing back on the sidewalk, she began to lift the jack-o'-lantern over her head.

The flame of the candle flickered crazily in the moonlight.

Elizabeth lifted it up—and up. Above her, she could see the moon floating in the sky. For a moment it looked as though it were on fire as well—

"Do it!" Betsy shouted, taking a step toward Elizabeth. "Or else!"

A strange war seemed to be going in within Elizabeth's chest. She shook her head hard and stared at the side of her house. Resolutely, Elizabeth raised the pumpkin above her head and took careful aim.

Sixteen

Jessica rounded a curve at top speed, sticking out a foot to keep herself from falling off the bike. She glanced at her watch. *Not much more time now. Please, let her be there!* Behind her, she could hear Steven coming closer and closer.

"We're about halfway up now, Jess," he wheezed. "Keep going, kid!"

Jessica stared at the moon, big and round in front of her now. *What was that?* Lifting one hand from the handlebars, she rubbed her eyes. *No, it couldn't be.*

"Jessica!" Steven barked. "Keep your eyes on the road!"

Had she swerved? Jessica looked down at the pavement, both eyes open now. She gulped. Her front wheel had come dangerously close to the edge of the road—and on this stretch of Courage Mountain, there wasn't much earth between the pavement and the cliff that overlooked the valley!

Steering back onto the road, Jessica looked up at the moon again. *No, I wasn't imagining it,* she thought faintly, gripping the handlebars as tightly as she could. The moon was burning. Great tongues of flame burst from somewhere deep inside it and lapped crazily around one another. The surface was completely invisible, hidden beneath the blazing fire. *It's like a huge lighted candle spinning in the sky,* Jessica thought. She could feel her breath coming in short gasps.

"Hurry up!" Steven called. He passed her, standing up on the pedals and pushing hard. "We don't have much time before the eclipse begins!"

Determined to shake the burning moon out of her mind, Jessica picked up speed. "I'm coming!" she cried to her brother. Then, to her shock and dismay, she caught sight of the reflector behind Steven's seat.

It looks just like the moon, she thought.
And it's on fire, too!

"Steven!" she cried, but Steven paid no attention. She closed her eyes for a moment, almost skidding off the road, and realized she could not escape—for the blazing moon was in her mind's eye, too.

Jessica dragged her bike to the side of the road. Clamping her eyes shut, she thrust both her arms in front of her face. *I've got to get rid of this picture*, she thought—but she couldn't. Even without using her eyes, she could still see the moon burning, burning in the sky, and molten bits of fiery rock beginning to drip down the sides to fall on—

To fall on what? Jessica concentrated as hard as she could. The picture in her mind was dim, and yet there was something awfully familiar about it.

My house.

My house, Jessica told herself again, her heart skipping a beat. *The fire from the moon is falling on my house!*

"Don't stop!" It was Steven's voice. Jessica's eyes snapped open. Steven was staring back at Jessica, a worried expression etched beneath his bike helmet. "Don't wimp out on me now!"

Jessica took a deep breath and shook her head. The image was gone.

"Coming," she called, and jumped back onto her bike. But as she rode on, a new image came into her head: Corrina's crescent moon.

She pictured the moon perfectly, and it seemed more real than anything—more real than Steven, more real than her bicycle, more real than the road, more real than Courage Mountain itself.

And Corrina's moon was crying.

Crying tears—hot, burning tears that didn't seem to stop coming.

And then it wasn't the crescent moon any longer but the face of Corrina herself.

It's a message, Jessica realized. *The moon and the fire—they're trying to tell me something. They're trying to tell me—*

Suddenly, Jessica understood what she had to do. "Steven!" she shouted, braking hard. A shower of gravel sailed up from the road.

Steven stopped, a scowl on his face. "What's up?" he asked.

"I—I—" Jessica's throat felt dry, but as she paused for breath, Corrina's tearstained face seemed more real than anything on earth. "I don't think they're coming," she blurted out, aware of how lame that must sound.

"Not coming?" Steven stared at her in disgust. "Didn't you talk to Betsy? Didn't you give Elizabeth that note like you said you would?"

"Uh-huh." Jessica shivered in the cold darkness. She didn't dare look back up at the moon. "I'm going to head back home."

"Why?" Steven demanded, putting his hands on his hips.

"Just because." *I can't explain it*, Jessica thought. *And you wouldn't understand it even if I could.* In her mind, the sobbing Corrina was changing into something new—a new face, but one Jessica recognized from Corrina's house.

Corrina's sister, she told herself with a shudder. *And the tears are getting hotter and hotter.*

"You go on," Jessica told Steven hastily. "Go. In case—just in case they show up."

Steven scowled. "Yeah, OK," he said, shaking his head. He leaped back onto his bike.

Wheeling her own bike around sharply, Jessica watched as Steven disappeared into the night ahead.

Clutching Jessica's pumpkin between her hands, Elizabeth threw it with all her might at the wall of the Wakefield house. "All right!" she could hear Betsy yell from behind her.

But Elizabeth scarcely heard. She stared at the pumpkin, which seemed to be flying in slow motion. As she watched, time stopped dead. The pumpkin spun onto its side. Elizabeth rubbed her eyes behind her mask. For a moment the pumpkin had looked exactly like a full moon.

I've seen this before, she told herself, straining to think back. *But where?*

Then, suddenly, the pumpkin was a pumpkin again, and time was moving at its usual speed. Elizabeth watched as Jessica's pumpkin hurtled toward the house and smashed firmly against it. The pumpkin broke into a dozen pieces, and the candle, still burning, landed in a pile of dead leaves by the side of the house.

"Yeah!" Betsy shouted. "All right, guys, this place is history. Let's crash that party now!"

Elizabeth stood silently, her gaze fixed on the pile of leaves. Where the candle had fallen, she could see a single leaf burning slowly. A thin wisp of smoke curled up from the pile.

"Wakefield!" Betsy's voice was loud. "You coming, or are you wimping out on us?"

Elizabeth could not speak. As she watched, a second leaf caught fire—and another—and another—and another. She moved her lips, but still the words would not come. There was a crackling sound, and two tiny sparks of flame shot up from the remains of Jessica's beautiful pumpkin.

"What's the matter with you?" Betsy demanded, coming closer to Elizabeth.

Staring at the hungry fire, Elizabeth could only shake her head. As she did so, she felt something she hadn't expected—

A single hot tear trickling down her cheek.

Jessica pedaled as hard as she could, not even slowing down for the curves. *If I fall, then I fall*, she told herself numbly. *I have to get home. If I can only make it there in time—*

In time for what?

Jessica didn't know. In her mind, Corrina's sister's face was now changing, too—*into Elizabeth's face.* And Elizabeth was crying, too, sobbing as though her heart would break, crying hotter and hotter tears—so hot that steam was beginning to rise from her cheeks.

Shaking away the image, Jessica snapped her head back to look over her shoulder.

The moon was beginning to disappear. Just a small section was missing from one side, but it was enough to make Jessica frantic. She choked back a sob.

Only a few minutes to go before the world is pitch black.

Elizabeth, she thought, her heart pounding with fear. *Elizabeth, my only sister, where are you?*

"Fire!" Betsy Martin shouted. "Run!"

Elizabeth strained to move, but she couldn't. Her feet seemed fastened to the ground. After a moment, there was nothing but silence from behind her. *They've gone and left me all alone,* she thought, watching as the flames rose higher.

Elizabeth couldn't run away. Her whole body felt heavy. *Those are my parents in that house,* she thought numbly. *My brother.*

Tears stung her eyes.

My—sister.

Above her, the eclipse had begun. As darkness covered more and more of the moon, Elizabeth felt something collapsing deep inside her heart. The flames grew wilder. Behind her mask, she pictured her family sleeping in their beds, unaware of the fire beginning to grow outside, and her chest began to heave.

This is my last chance, she told herself, straining to get her legs to move. But she couldn't move a muscle.

In the gathering darkness, Elizabeth began to cry.

Jessica looked frantically up into the sky, narrowly missing a station wagon that barreled by her, tires screeching. The moon was more than half gone.

Where is she? she wondered desperately.

Her chest heaved with the effort of pedaling. She reached up to wipe some moisture from her cheek, and in a flash Jessica realized that the tears she was imagining on Elizabeth's face weren't Elizabeth's at all—but Jessica's own.

Seventeen

Oh, no! Jessica thought as she came riding up to the Wakefield house and skidded to a stop. A fire was beginning to rage—and Elizabeth was standing nearby, crying desperately.

Without saying a word, Jessica ditched the bike, leaving the wheels spinning crazily. She ran to Elizabeth and gave her sister a quick hug. Then she raced to the back of the house, she grabbed the garden hose. Her fingers felt about twelve sizes too large as she tried to turn on the faucet full blast. The first two times she couldn't turn the faucet at all. The third time the water coughed—and then began to shoot from the end of the hose.

Carrying the hose in front of her, Jessica ran around to the front again and aimed the water onto the fire. *I only hope it's not too high already,* she told herself grimly. The water sizzled as it fell onto the flames. *Come on*, Jessica urged it silently. *Come on!*

Jessica knew that the last sliver of moon was disappearing. She stole a glance at her sister's face, hidden by the mask. *It's time, Lizzie*, she pleaded, concentrating on sending a message to her twin. *This is it. It's now or—*

The flames leaped higher, and Jessica realized she wasn't paying enough attention to the fire. Stepping forward, she sprayed the water all over the pile: dried leaves, she saw, mixed with what she recognized as the remains of her own pumpkin.

The fire sputtered. Jessica stole a look upward. As she watched, the tiniest bit of moon glowed in the sky for the briefest of moments—and then all was dark.

She turned to her sister. Elizabeth's body had gone limp. With an effort that seemed to exhaust her completely, Elizabeth reached up and pulled the mask off her face.

The remains of the fire lapped at the edge of the lawn. Jessica ached to help her sister, but remembered Corrina's words—*Elizabeth is the only one who can save herself*. She watched as Elizabeth clenched and unclenched her fingers. Then, with an angry, determined motion, Elizabeth wadded up the awful mask and flung it violently into the fire.

There was a sizzling sound as the flames licked

around the outside of the mask, and then a bursting sound as the inside caught on fire as well, and then the cold, dark air was filled with a terrible smell of burning—and the next thing Jessica knew, her sister had leaped into her arms and was crying hysterically.

With one arm, Jessica clutched her twin as hard as she could. With the other, she trained the hose on the fire until the last ember was out and the first sliver of moon had peeked back into the sky. Jessica braced herself and looked up.

It wasn't red this time.

And it wasn't on fire.

It was the same old, normal moon she'd seen for years before this whole awful business had started. Jessica closed her eyes, gently at first, then more firmly. The only picture she got this time was Corrina's crescent moon. Grinning, as usual.

Or perhaps a little more than usual.

Jessica sighed deeply in the cool night air and turned to her sister.

The hair around Elizabeth's face was wet with her tears. "Oh, Jess—I'm—I'm so sorry!" she stammered.

"Shhh," Jessica said soothingly, brushing away the hair from her sister's face. "Hey, Lizzie?" she began gently. "Let's be a two-headed sea monster next Halloween, OK?"

*   *   *

"I don't know how to thank you, Corrina," Jessica said with feeling.

It was Saturday morning, and she and Elizabeth were sitting on Corrina's old couch sipping iced tea. Corrina sat in her usual chair, a smile on her face.

"Actually, *I'm* the one that should be thanking you," Elizabeth put in, leaning forward. "If you hadn't done so much to help Jessica, I'd be—I'd be—well, I don't know what I'd be!" She shuddered.

Jessica frowned. "Are you positive that the mask won't come back again?" she asked uncertainly. "I know I saw it burn and everything, and this morning we spread out the ashes and buried them, just to be safe, but—"

Corrina shook her head. "We can hope," she said. "But I'm afraid, my dear, that we can never be sure."

"I'll never know how you got there when you did," Elizabeth added, reaching for her sister's hand. "Just lucky, I guess."

Luck had nothing to do with it, Jessica thought, squeezing Elizabeth's hand back. She winced as she remembered the images that had flashed through her mind that night—the moon a ball of fire, Corrina's crescent crying, and then Elizabeth's own face. *Luck? Yeah, right!* Out of the corner of her eye, Jessica could see Corrina wink at her sympathetically.

She knows all about it, Jessica told herself with a rueful grin. Somehow she wasn't surprised.

Corrina stood up and stretched. "I'm going to get some more iced tea," she announced. "Would you girls like some?"

"No, thank you," Elizabeth said, as Jessica shook her head.

"Very well," Corrina told them. "I'll be right back." She vanished into the kitchen.

"She's an amazing person," Elizabeth murmured, watching her go.

"She sure is," Jessica agreed. "You know, we should really do something to show our appreciation."

Elizabeth smiled. "Maybe we could offer to weed her garden," she said eagerly.

"I'll see if I can get that old lawn mower working again, and maybe I can clean out all the leaves that are blocking those gutters," Jessica added.

"And we can bake her cookies every week," Elizabeth said, jumping in, "and give the house a good coat of paint—"

"And vacuum once in a while," Jessica interrupted, "and buy her some new lights."

Elizabeth giggled. "It's funny to see you getting excited about doing *work*."

Jessica tossed her hair with a grin. "Yeah, well, I can be pretty helpful when I want to."

"Believe me, I know!" Elizabeth laughed. "But seriously, Jess, we might not manage to get all that work done. Let's just say that we'll visit her as often as we can."

Jessica nodded. "Good idea." *Elizabeth's right*, she told herself. *We'll do what we can, but visiting's most important of all.* She stared up at the portraits above the mantelpiece. "There's only one thing that's still bothering me," she went on. "Who had the mask before?"

Elizabeth frowned. "What do you mean?"

"There was a fire," Jessica said slowly, "and everyone in Corrina's family was killed, except Corrina. What I want to know is, did the mask turn Corrina's sister evil—or did it turn Corrina herself evil?"

Elizabeth looked up at the portraits. "I don't know," she said, shaking her head. "But you know what I think?"

"What?" Jessica asked.

Elizabeth took a sip of tea. "I think you should let it alone. I think Corrina would have told you if she'd wanted you to know."

Jessica sighed. Elizabeth was just so *thoughtful* sometimes.

Then again, Jessica wouldn't want her any other way.

Corrina bustled back into the room and sat down beneath the portraits. "I'm sorry about your Halloween," she said. "But there will be another one next year, won't there?"

"It was worth it," Jessica said quickly. "I'd give up a hundred Halloweens to get rid of that curse."

"A hundred?" Elizabeth grinned.

Well, maybe not a hundred. "Thanksgiving's next," Jessica pointed out. "That's kind of fun, too."

"Not as good as Halloween, but not bad, either," Elizabeth agreed. "Let's see—" A mischievous look came into her eye as she stared at Jessica. "Turkey bells, turkey bells, turkey all the way!" she sang out.

"Elizabeth!" Jessica cried, rising from her seat.

"What, you don't like my singing?" Elizabeth demanded.

Jessica sank back down and gave her sister a fierce hug. "I'm so glad you're back," she said.

Bantam Books in the SWEET VALLEY TWINS series.
Ask your bookseller for the books you have missed.